my star, my love

(an eversea series novella)

NATASHA BOYD

My Star, My Love
Copyright © 2014 by Natasha Boyd

Interior Design by Angela McLaurin, Fictional Formats
https://www.facebook.com/FictionalFormats

my star, my love

(an eversea series novella)

NATASHA BOYD

one

"OH MY GOD, I can't do this," I choked out as the car neared the airport turn off. Panic had me by the throat. It was also hanging on my limbs and doing an ice bucket challenge in my gut. "Seriously, I can't."

Jack's green eyes were fixed on me, luminous in spite of the dim interior of the town car we'd taken to the airport. His brow furrowed. "Okay, just breathe, baby. Keri Ann, just breathe."

Damn, I thought I was over this. My anxiety about the fact I was about to embark on a twelve-hour flight over a rather large and deep body of water known as the Atlantic wasn't helped by present circumstances. I was still not okay with the odd photographer trying desperately to get a picture of us together, but now there were three of them standing impatiently by curbside check-in at Atlanta Hartsfield-Jackson International Airport. How were they always one step ahead of us?

Kill. Me. Now.

"I'm sorry I'm such a head case," I managed and dropped my eyes to his firm *Rag and Bone*-clad thighs as he instructed our driver to do a circuit of the airport terminals. "I swear, I must have been a kamikaze bomber in World War Two or something. It always feels like a one-way trip where landing gear will never be used. Why am I so afraid of flying?"

Jack chuckled, the smooth rasp and rumble was like popping an antianxiety med; it was instantly calming. I closed my eyes to let his sound wash over me. He'd been so distracted the last few weeks.

I'd been driven instead of flying on my own to meet Jack for our connecting flight to England. *To meet his mother!* Even when we met today, he'd seemed preoccupied. Hearing him laugh though, and at least try and calm my nerves, helped.

We hadn't seen each other in two weeks, him having to be back in Los Angeles for meetings, and me finishing up my semester at the Savannah College of Art and Design. The car he'd ordered to drive me the five hours to Atlanta had met him at a private airfield north of the city, and we hadn't had a chance to be alone yet.

"Are you sure it's not because you're meeting my mother?" Jack teased.

I sighed, the breath catching over my tension.

As soon as we were moving again, he leaned over, dosing me with his piney scent and bringing his gorgeous lips so close to mine my heart tripped. He unsnapped my seatbelt. "Come here," he said and hauled me roughly onto his lap. He worked my knee over him, his hand feeling hot through my linen cargo pants, until I sat astride him on the back seat. His arm pulled me tight against his body, our foreheads touching.

This was a good way to distract myself from impending doom. I'd pick death by Jack any day of the week.

I curled my fingers into the soft hair at his nape and scraped my nails up into his hairline like I knew he liked.

"Careful," he whispered with a sexy smirk, eyes glittering. "I've missed you far too much." Then his arms left me to mess with his seatbelt and stretch it around us both.

I laughed quietly as he grimaced and grunted and finally clicked it into place, locking me tight against him.

"Safety first. Damn, we should always travel like this with you strapped against me."

I was saved answering as the car took a speed bump a little too fast and bounced us.

Holy hell.

"You're hard," I squeaked, and my insides did a zipline over hot boiling lava, the heat wafting through me. "Did the driver hear that?" I whispered with a cringe of embarrassment. What was I saying? Of course he did.

"You sound surprised. Has it not been apparently obvious that I have no control of my body when you're around?" Jack's laughing tone slid back into a whisper as he dropped my gaze and angled his lips for my ear.

I shivered. *Me neither* I answered mentally.

"Let alone when you're pretty much wrapped around me. And sitting right on my—"

"Sir?" the driver's voice cut in, his tone vapidly neutral as his training required. "We're approaching the terminal again. Are we stopping this time?"

I sighed and pulled back reluctantly, resting my forefinger over Jack's soft lips. Such a contrast to the rough surrounding skin that was already sprouting its shadow. "Yes, we're getting out. Sorry," I said, feeling it was my place to assert that I was pulling myself together. And Jack had successfully refocused my mind. As he always did.

We adjusted the seatbelt and I slid back over to my side. "Are *you* okay that I'm meeting your mother?" I asked. *Oh why did I ask that?*

Jack smiled tightly as the car approached the curb again, and the driver hopped out. "Of course." Then glancing out the window as he mashed his maroon ball cap on his head, he muttered, "Showtime." His street side door opened, letting in the whine of jet engines and chattering people.

"Jack!" A male voice called his name.

He slid out and the driver closed the door behind him,

leaving me a blessed moment's peace before he came round to get me. I had seconds to slide on my large sunglasses and steel my nerves. I did a quick scan of my wardrobe choice: my Snapper Grill T-shirt worn for nostalgia and my festive red Chuck Taylors, and looked for stray toilet paper or anything that might embarrass me. All good.

God, my life. The last eight months since Jack and I had hit the tabloids with Audrey Lane's awful story, claiming that Jack's cheating had caused her to miscarry their baby, had been awful. Spectacularly happy because Jack and I were together, but trying to start studying for a degree while essentially living under a microscope, was tough. But Jack had been right. The tabloid fever had only lasted so long, and then they were bored when Jack wasn't around. I wasn't quite as interesting to them on my own. Thank goodness. But when we were together? Different story.

It had been tough to make friends at college because everyone whispered about me. But when the tabloid furor finally died down, and after I was assigned a study group and got to know some of my fellow students one on one, it was better.

The door opened and Jack held out his hand. We moved hastily, pausing side by side for just a moment with big smiles to have our picture taken. Our driver, after handing off our luggage to the airport porter, walked ahead of us, clearing a path and leaving the small group of photographers behind. It was comforting to know he had bodyguard training. Inside the terminal, we were led directly to the crew check-in and met with a personal assistant from the airline. Jack and I shook our driver's hand, thanking him, and then we were hurried down a quiet hallway of the airport, leaving our luggage to be privately screened and checked. It was ironic that I'd never taken a regular flight like most people. My first airplane experience was a private jet with Jack, and now we were "going commercial" as Jack termed it, and I knew it was hardly the procedure most people went through.

He wrapped a hand around my waist, hauling me close as we walked. Before long we came to double security doors where a middle-aged and efficient looking woman in the navy airline uniform met us and handed me my purse and our passports. The doors led out to a public area where a crowd of harried travelers walked, marched, or flat out ran in all different directions. "I guess we skipped the security line," I murmured to Jack.

There was a golf cart looking thing we jumped on. It beeped, letting people know to move, earning a few curious glances. Jack pretended to study the inside of his passport to keep from looking up, and the bill of his cap kept his face mostly hidden. He was a pro at this.

We sped past people, gates, and a newsstand I would have loved to stop at and buy a book. Finally, we pulled down a carpeted side hall. Here two large frosted glass double doors indicated a First Class Lounge. But we didn't stop. We went ten feet beyond that to a smaller innocuous white door. I raised my eyebrow at Jack in a silent question.

"VIP room. More privacy," he whispered.

More VIP than first class. Alrighty, then.

JACK HANDED ME a package shaped like a large brick that he withdrew from his backpack. Not quite long enough to be a shoebox and heavier than that. It was wrapped in red paper, the folded ends, messy and irregular, puffy from being folded over itself so many times, and taped closed with far too much tape. "Did Katie wrap this for you?" I asked, just to see his reaction.

We were sitting in two club chairs in a corner of the lounge partially obscured from the entrance by a frosted screen. I'd just eaten smoked salmon on tiny little miniature toasts and was nursing my second glass of champagne from the ice bucket in the corner Jack insisted I have to calm my nerves. And no one had bothered us since we'd been offered refreshments, which in and of itself was a miracle. We'd been apart for weeks, but I didn't feel we were quite alone enough to start making up for lost time.

"What? The perfect angles and lack of excess paper gave

it away?" He snorted and rolled his eyes, his dimple making an appearance.

I laughed softly. "Anyway, it's nine days until Christmas. What are you doing giving me my present this early?"

"This isn't your present. This is the twelve days of Christmas. Days one through three since I haven't seen you until today."

I furrowed my brow. Intriguing. Three gifts in one.

"Hurry up," Jack said, impatiently.

I grinned at him, amused by his boyish attitude. "I think you're more excited about this gift than—"

"Open it!"

"Okay, okay." I laughed and tore open one end to reveal what looked like three hardbacks stacked together and quickly pulled at the rest of the paper. Surprise and wonder stopped my hands as I stared down at the cover of the first hardback. *Warriors of Erath: Dream Warrior.* The cover was the original. Wait. I quickly glanced up at Jack to see his face broken out into a massive heart-stopping and self-satisfied grin. He was seemingly relaxed, slouching in his black T-shirt, his strong forearms resting along each chair arm, but his long fingers drummed incessantly, belying his impatience. Looking down again, I flipped the book open and thumbed through the first few pages until I found what I was looking for.

First Edition. 10-1

I let out a sharp breath. "Wow," I said in shock. I'd wanted this forever and constantly stalked eBay to that end. A first printing of a first edition. I swallowed hard, suddenly overwhelmed. "Thank you. How on earth did you—"

"Wait, keep going. Turn the page," he said as I went to put them aside and thank him properly before even looking at the next in the stack.

I paused and reopened the book, heading to the title page.

To Keri Ann, the girl who captured
the heart of the real dream warrior:
Keep believing in your dreams.
Your dreams believe in you.
Warmest regards,
JM Burke

The message blurred as my eyes filled with tears.

"Oh God, don't cry," Jack whispered earnestly and pulled the books out of my hands, laying them on the floor. He hauled me onto his lap, where I went willingly.

Burying my wet face in his delicious neck, I curled into a ball, hiking up my knees too and cursed my ridiculous and sentimental heart. "Sorry, they're happy tears," I murmured against his warm skin and followed it with a kiss to the soft spot under his ear. I held him tightly, his body hard and hot beneath my hands, and focused on his heartbeat. The pulse in his throat. "I love you so much," I whispered. *Understatement.* I adored this guy. I loved him with my entire being. My heart swelled so huge when I let myself think of him, of us; it was physically painful. In the best way.

A small shudder went through him, and his hands tightened on me, his head dropping forward. "I can't wait to be truly alone with you, to hold you all night."

"Me too. And I can show you how much I love my presents," I whispered in his ear, biting back a grin because I knew what was coming.

Jack let out a low vibrating growl and shifted beneath me. "Wench," he said.

I pulled back with a giggle and took his face in my hands.

His eyes stared into mine.

We said nothing and everything.

two

FOR SOME REASON, I'd been lulled into the feeling we were escaping madness when we left America. And in the quiet cocoon of first class, each of us with our own flat bed, although Jack came and spooned with me while we watched a movie, I'd gotten over the fact we were flying in a steel tube thirty thousand feet above the ocean. I'd succumbed to the mindless drone of the engines and warm curve of Jack at my back and fallen asleep. It was only when he gently shook me awake an hour before landing that he spilled the beans about the paparazzi in England.

"Hey Keri Ann, baby, wake up. They're going to ask us to sit upright for landing. Have some breakfast."

"I can't eat right now, it's," I grumbled and looked at my watch through bleary eyes, "two thirty in the morning." I pulled the small but cozy white airline duvet over my head and felt Jack laughing next to me as he climbed onto my bed.

"It's seven thirty, we need to change the time on your watch." He lifted the cover so he could slide his hand over my belly, making me sigh with sleepy pleasure. "Tomorrow," he whispered in my ear, "I'll be able to wake you up with more incentive."

"What? With a real almond croissant from Pret A Manger?" I joked, deliberately ignoring his sensual undertone. I'd had one back in October when Jack and I had spent a weekend in New York. Knowing it was an import from London had put me on a mission to have an original pretty much as soon as we landed.

Jack stroked my hair back from my face. "We'll get you one of those as soon as possible, I promise. Right now you gotta wake up, and we have to talk about what we may face out there when we get off the plane."

I groaned. "You go. I'll just come off the plane incognito later, and you can pick me up."

He was quiet so long, I finally flicked my eyes open and rolled over toward him.

Resting his head on his hand, his elbow propped, Jack gazed down at me with his eyes grey green in the odd, bright airplane light. His hair was messy, and I reached up to smooth it down. "I'm sorry," I whispered. "I didn't mean that. I'll be by your side."

"I know it's hard for you. It's fine if you want to do that."

"No. What is the plan? I have a feeling I'll screw it up if we don't go together."

"Come on, get up. I'll have them bring you some breakfast while you freshen up, bathrooms free, then I'll fill you in."

He dropped a lingering kiss on my lips and a short one on the tip of my nose, then uncurled himself from me.

WE WERE HUSTLED off the plane first, and like our departure, we were met by an airline rep who escorted us through the crew and diplomatic passport line. Our bags were handled for us and would be delivered later in the day. Jack kept his ball cap and glasses on, but they were so trademark, everyone stared at him anyway.

The hard part was entering the arrivals hall. Yep. Photographers. Lots of them, and lots of flashes. And lewd and crude questions.

One voice, a loud, guttural British accent, maybe Cockney, though I wasn't familiar with the different dialects, was an incessant stream of questions about Jack's shenanigans the last time he was here and if I would mind if he looked up a few old girlfriends.

Jack vibrated with tension next to me as we walked swiftly, heads down, following the rep who was now joined by a stocky guy in a suit who Jack seemed to know. I assumed he was our driver, and a security guard. They were on either side, guiding us. It was when that awful guy yelled something after us about the waitress having a magic *something too crude to mention*, that I felt Jack almost snap. He hissed and pulled me tight against him and stopped.

It was so abrupt I stumbled and we all came to an awkward pause, the general throng also quieting down. "Take a deep breath," I whispered. "Please get us out of here." Jack's mouth was tight, but a split second later he nodded, and we kept moving.

We finally got outside into a bitingly cold early morning wind and dived into the warm leather interior of a black Range Rover.

"Okay, so that car behind us will stop anyone following us, and we're trading cars in the parking garage. Or so they think," Jack informed me as I craned my neck back to look. Sure enough a black sedan pulled out behind us and followed us to a parking entrance where it came to a stop sideways, blocking anyone from following. We drove in and parked next to a silver version of our same car also with tinted windows. The driver got out and headed around to make like he was opening back doors. "We just stay here."

I could tell it probably looked like we were trading cars if anyone was able to see in from the entrance, which I'm sure they were. "I don't understand why we don't actually do it. Surely most of them still think we left in a black car? Won't they still follow this one?"

"They are all talking to each other. They coordinate for the most part, even though they are competition. It's a total sport here, worse than any other country. They'll work together, and then get cutthroat about the pictures. At this point they are just trying to find out where we're headed by sending a single 'follow car' so they can get pictures later. It's the follow car I want to avoid."

Swallowing, I stared out the window to the parking entrance. This was insane. I thought it had been crazy back home. The feel of Jack's warm hand on my cheek had me peeling my wide eyes away from the back window to look at him. He'd removed his sunglasses and gently took mine off. "You okay?" he asked.

I nodded and leaned into his hand. "Are you?"

He sighed. "Yes. No. God, I hate it here." His hand left my face, and he turned to face forward. The driver got back in and we started moving. "Welcome back, Mr. Eversea," the driver said with a curiously amused tone. He was maybe mid thirties, portly, with slicked back brown hair.

"Nigel," Jack greeted him. "When are you going to start calling me Jack?"

Suddenly aware of the delicious smell of warm coffee, I leaned forward inhaling loudly. "Coffee. Well, that's just cruel."

Jack's shoulders relaxed and he chuckled. "Nigel. This is—"

"Keri Ann, I know. Lovely to meet you, finally. I see this boy finally got 'is heart back." Nigel, craned his thick neck up and winked at me in the rearview mirror.

I turned to look at Jack and he looked at Nigel, avoiding my silent question. "Nah, she still has it. Owns it. Doubt I'll be getting it back anytime soon."

"Ah well, at least it's next to you and not on the other side of the world."

I folded my arms, amused. "I'm right here, guys. I'm not an inanimate vessel." Huffing, I pretended to be annoyed but was ridiculously warmed that Jack had obviously spoken of me the last time he was here, which was back when I thought he'd moved on and forgotten me.

"Cranky," Jack teased.

"If we don't stop for coffee soon, Nigel will get to experience just how cranky I can get."

Nigel reached down with his left hand and pulled up a carry container. "Oh my God," I squeaked. "Is that coffee for me? I love you!" I leaned forward, carefully taking the carrier with two paper cups from his hand.

"Bit fair weather with 'er heart, this one," Nigel said to Jack with a laugh.

I handed a cup to Jack and took the one that said milk, two sugars. "Thank you, both," I breathed, touched that Jack had even told Nigel how I liked my coffee. Taking a careful sip, I leaned back and closed my eyes, savoring the taste. I'd always liked coffee but had become a bit of a junkie since I started college and had to work at crazy times to get studio time and projects done.

The time change to England was a killer. My legs felt like lead. "I could sleep for an epoch," I muttered with a sigh.

Jack reached over and smoothed my hair off my temple. "We have to try and stay awake 'til this evening, otherwise jet lag will kick our asses, and it'll be worse tomorrow."

"I'm guessing you've both known each other a while?" I asked, looking between Jack and Nigel. Maybe Jack used the same driver on all his trips here.

"Turns out I've known this runt since he was eight," Nigel answered my question with a chuckle. "Though, only found out he'd become this Hollywood hotshot earlier this year. I've been working for a car service for about seven years now and was just back from holiday last January and staying with my aunt, and she says to me, 'you remember little William and 'is mum what came to live with us all them years ago? You'll never guess who he's become,' she says. I says, 'don't tell me… a car salesman.' She's like, 'guess again.' And I do. It bloody goes on for about twenty minutes, doesn't it?" He checked the mirror and changed lanes.

I glanced at Jack with a bemused smile and he winked. "Is he talking about Mrs. Eversea whose name you borrowed?"

Jack nodded.

Nigel went on. "Then she's like 'warmer, colder.' 'Cor blimey,' I says. 'The bloody Easter bunny, I don't know.'"

I busted out laughing and Jack snorted.

"'Just tell me already, I'm getting irritated now, you know?' She says, '… well, he's that chap what's in the films in't he?'" he mimicked her high pitched voice. "So I says, 'but Aunty, could you narrow it down a bit?' She says, 'you know the one about the dreams and the twin brothers, they're like these gladiator types, but not. *You* know,' she says. And bloody hell, if I didn't. 'Jack Eversea,' I say, like she's half a biscuit short on 'er tea. 'But he's a yank,' I say. 'And that's *your* surname. You telling me that's not a coincidence?' Thought she was finally off her rocker, I did."

Jack laughed. "Well, I knew Mrs. Eversea's nephew was a driver for a car service," he said to me. "And I needed someone I could trust. So… here we are."

"Yep. Here we are," Nigel echoed. "Even if he's not an Everton supporter like me. You can't be *too* perfect, now can you?"

Jack rolled his eyes good-naturedly.

"Everton?" I asked.

"A soccer club," Jack filled in, then looked back at Nigel. "Funnily enough, I hear people are calling them *Eversea* though, now that you've gone and bought all those Chelsea players. Can't find your own talent then?"

I felt the brakes tap on the car. "You better watch your mouth, William, or I'll turf you out on the side of the M25," Nigel shot back, using Jack's real childhood name.

"That was low, Nigel. Watch it or I'll tell your aunt about—"

"All right, all right," Nigel groused.

The misty, drizzly morning made it hard to see much outside beyond the highway, though I saw glimpses of green fields and the odd line of semi-detached row houses here and there.

"So what are we doing then? Are we going straight to your mom's?" A sign said we were leaving the M25 and taking an exit toward the M4. The mist was clearing in patches. It was true that everything in England was really green. It was a deep wet green made more vibrant for being set against the grey overcast sky.

"We'll go tomorrow. I'm having Nige take us to the Four Seasons in Hampshire."

Nigel cleared his throat. "You know she's expecting you."

"I know."

I turned back to the better view of my superstar boyfriend. How did he possibly look this good after traveling for twenty-four hours? He had to be tired.

"Let's go, Jack," I said, my tone low. I knew his mom must be so excited to see him. "Besides, if we stay at a hotel, we have more chance of being discovered, and we might accidentally lead them to your mom when we leave tomorrow."

Jack placed a hand above my knee, the heat radiating through to my skin. He leaned in close to my ear, his breath tickling my nerves and raising bumps on my flesh. "But I've missed you," he whispered. "And there's things I want to do with you that are probably going to make you scream."

My body's reaction was instantaneous and overwhelming. I flicked my eyes to Nigel in the drivers seat. He was oblivious, thank God. If he'd looked up right then, he'd see a girl with her blood beating thick and heavy, causing flushed skin and glassy eyes. I squirmed on the seat and pressed my lips closed to avoid emitting any sound whatsoever, earning a chuckle from Jack.

"You see?" He arched a cocky eyebrow over teasing but heated eyes, and his hand ran slowly up my thigh.

I narrowed my eyes at him. *Arrogant*, I said in my head.

Confident, his green eyes argued.

Regardless, I still thought we should go straight there.

Nigel turned the car, and we all chatted as the vehicle ate up the miles.

I was nervous about meeting Jack's mom, but part of me couldn't wait. I just hoped she liked *me*.

"She's gonna love you. Stop worrying," Jack said.

"I'm not."

"You are," he said and brushed his thumb over my bottom lip, releasing it from the grip of my teeth.

I scowled. "I'm not worrying, I'm hopped up on caffeine, have hardly slept, swoon-effect, and I'm hungry."

"Swoon-effect?" Jack inquired, not missing how I'd snuck that in there.

He didn't need to know what happened inside my body every time I saw him. "Long story," I muttered.

Jack grinned impishly. "Do you want your gift for day five of the twelve days of Christmas?"

"You have a gift with you right now? Uh, sure. Wait, not to be a spoiled brat, but what happened to day four?"

Jack winked and shrugged. "That was me. My presence is your present and all that."

Rolling my eyes, I shook my head, laughing. Nigel was doing the same.

Jack briefly rubbed his hands together and leaned forward to get something Nigel was handing back to him. "Day five. Something you've been craving, apart from me—" he added.

I let out a snort.

A box. A white bakery box with a familiar red logo on it.

Ooooh, heaven.

"Oh my God, if this is what I think it is…" Taking the box gently from his hands, I laid it on my lap and opened the lid to a view of golden brown, perfectly flaky pastries sprinkled with toasted almonds and powdered sugar. It was. "Mmmmmm," I breathed. "Thank you." I offered one to Jack, and Nigel, then finally bit into one myself, feeling the flaky pillow give under my teeth and warm almond filling and fresh buttery croissant surround my taste buds. So good. I let out a long, deep groan.

Opening my eyes, I found Jack staring at me, his eyes dark. Chewing quickly, I swallowed. "What?"

"Nigel?" he raised his voice, his eyes not leaving me.

"Yes, sir?"

"Do you have any music you can put on? I'm about to snog my girl here, and I doubt you want to be listening to us."

"Jack!" Hot embarrassment pumped blood to my cheeks.

"Blimey." Nigel chuckled. "You'd think you hadn't seen each other instead of just arrivin' together."

"Er, we haven't," Jack said with a smirk, his eyes settling on my lips. "I've been in California, and Keri Ann's been busy at college in Savannah."

"Ah. Other side of the country is it? Right-o. I'll put some Coldplay on."

"You do that. Make it loud."

I glared at Jack, mortified, but with a sting of anticipation swirling through my lower belly.

"Relax, baby," he soothed. "Snogging is just slang for kissing." He leaned forward and moved the box off my lap to the floor before sliding his hand around my head and into my hair. "With tongue," he added.

three

WHEN JACK KISSED, it was a melody rushing through me. The build of a chorus that thrummed in my blood and beat in my chest, my body at one with the resonance as it built, layer upon layer, like a song one could feel more than hear.

I didn't just taste the sweet almond and coffee taste on his tongue that rode like white caps on the flavor that was uniquely Jack. I was in the cathedral of Jack. His presence surrounded me with perfect architecture to take the burning want he created with every slide of his mouth and every tightening of his hands holding me to him, soaring and whipping around me until I was trembling with the force of it. And flying along side it. Along side him.

"Christ on a broomstick, do you think you could tone it down just a bit?" Nigel's voice tore through the music like the needle off a record. "It's not one of them fancy cars I can just raise the partition and turn the bloody noise off. Don't you think that was enough to tide you over?"

My chest heaved, and Jack exhaled a rough laugh.

"Anyway," Nigel added, shaking his head, "we're here. So straighten yourselves up and think of England. The green and glorious land."

I WAS IN a storybook. There were fields as far as I could see in the grey misty morning with low, stone walls and small skeletal copses of bare winter trees here and there. The car had left the highway and meandered up a narrow tarred lane that passed through a village consisting of a pub, *The Goat in Boots,* one or two other businesses, a small church, and a shiny bright red cylindrical "post box." Christmas wreaths and pine garlands adorned doors and lampposts. Then the "village" was gone and the fields stretched out again.

Rising up a small hill, we slowed by a break in the stone wall with a wooden sign that read "The Grange." We turned in and drove down a winding gravel driveway, bordered by strategically high hedges until we came out in front of a pretty two-story but small rectangle building. I couldn't make out the masonry, not quite stone or brick, but not stucco either; it was tawny brown in coloring. A wild tangle of thorny limbs covered most of one half of the facade and eased around the doorframe.

"Roses," said Jack. "They're incredible when they bloom." I'd bet they were. The whole place was so very pretty despite the miserable day and the bare winter feel. A large fir wreath with a red bow hung on the wooden door that suddenly flew open.

A short and slender lady, with dark glossy hair, dressed in jeans, green rubber boots, and a cream knitted sweater, came bounding out of the house, her mouth cracked wide with a huge smile.

Jack squeezed my hand, then opened the door and climbed out just in time to catch the woman in an airborne hug that had him swinging her round to the side with her momentum. His "mum."

I smiled at her excitement and the sound of Jack's rumble of a laugh while my heart pounded with nerves. Cold, damp air hit my bare arms as I shifted to Jack's seat to exit after him.

He set his mom down and turned back to me, reaching out a hand. His smile was the most brilliant sight. It was clear he adored his mother. I glanced at her nervously as I climbed out.

"Mum…" Jack seemed to have lost his words.

We all seemed stuck in a moment.

I swallowed nervously as she gazed at me. Exactly my height, her eyes were just like Jack's but darker, and she was absolutely beautiful. So much like Jack but softer. Her face bore pale smile lines and crows feet at her eyes that told me they crinkled often. Her dark hair was glossy and softly pulled back. Then she reached out and took my hand, pulling me into a tight hug. The scent of warm cooking and Christmas spices surrounded me, her sweater soft under my arms, and I squeezed my eyes closed at the sudden rush of emotion— relief and love for a lady I'd never met before flooded my system. After a moment, we pulled apart, and she held me at arms length. "Keri Ann," she said in a stunning British accent, and I wanted to melt. "It's lovely to meet you. I'm Charlotte."

"Nice to meet you." I smiled, my eyes suspiciously watery and my nerves evaporating into the morning mist.

Jack, smiling, took my hand again, threading his fingers through mine.

Tiredness and lack of warm clothing made me shiver in the chilly winter morning.

"Gracious, it's freezing, and you're both in T-shirts. Where on earth is your luggage? Hurry inside. Go sit by the Aga and warm up, and we'll have a spot of tea. I can't believe you came straight here! I'm thrilled. Go on with you." She motioned toward the house then turned to Nigel who was waiting quietly by the car after taking our hand luggage out. "Hi Nigel, darling. Will you stay and have some tea?" Well, now that we'd had a split second of awkward silence it seemed Charlotte was making up for lost talking time.

Jack let go of my hand and slung his arm around my shoulders. Pulling me in tight, he kissed the top of my head and then guided me toward the front door. "Come on." He was positively radiating giddiness, and I nestled into his glow and let him lead me into another part of his life.

Stepping through the low front door, Jack had to duck slightly.

"People used to be way smaller in the old days," I surmised. "How old is this place?"

The flagstone floor was worn and uneven, even undulating into smooth dips that were almost bowl-like in their shape. The smell of wood polish and waxed rain jackets met us just inside, and the walls were a mix of gleaming wood paneling in parts and whitewashed plaster in others.

"I don't know. A couple hundred years maybe? It was a farmhouse. Kind of still is, if you count my mum's chickens and her gardening. Most of the fields that used to be with this house were sold to surrounding farms though."

Walking farther into the dim glow of the interior, the smell morphed into something deliciously edible, spiced with cinnamon and clove. The lighting came from a few leaded glass windows and some lamps, as there didn't seem to be any overhead lights anywhere. I had stepped back in time almost. It was so cozy and comforting inside, I felt like I'd crawled into a gorgeous warm blanket at the end of an icy trek.

Jack led me down a short hall to a large spacious kitchen that was lighter than the front part of the house. The back wall was a series of windows, obviously newer but in keeping with the style of the home. A large farm table dwarfed the room. On the other side of it stood the source of all the heat: an old-fashioned Aga oven with a warm cream finish stood proudly against the far wall.

"Wow," I said, letting go of Jack's hand and walking around the table. "I think this is an original." And the source of the delicious Christmas smell, I believed.

"It looks like it. But I bought it for Mum last year when her old one finally gave up. She almost refused. Didn't want me spending that on her. But, I won." He grinned.

"It's stunning." Having looked at them online over the last few years while dreaming of Butler family home renovations, I knew how expensive they were. I saw the kettle off to the side and placed it on the burner closest to me.

Jack came around and stopped close behind me. His hands settled on my waist and then slipped around my belly.

He dropped his head forward onto my shoulder. "Thank you," he breathed.

"For?" I asked, folding my arms over his to keep him against me as I settled my head back against him.

"Making us come straight here." He turned his face and pressed his mouth under my ear, making me shiver. "Being here with me at all. Doing all of this with me. Being in my life. Being you." His mouth found my skin again, his voice husky.

"Well, me too. Thank you for bringing me here. Your mom, she's…" I swallowed against a hard ball that suddenly seemed stuck in my throat. My eyes stung. Well, she was a mother. His mother. She adored her child.

And she loved me because he did.

And really? Love and beauty just seemed to radiate off her. I didn't realize how much I missed the feeling of being loved like that by a mother, or grandmother, whom I adored and respected. It suddenly blindsided me. Nostalgia, not so much for my own mom, but Nana, slid over me. But my own mother too. I squeezed Jack's arms tighter around me. I was so grateful he had her. With everything he'd been exposed to growing up, she'd protected him as best she could. Made him who he was today. "She's beautiful," I finally finished thickly, quietly.

"PINK?" I LAUGHED, meeting the mirth in Charlotte's eyes. "Tell me you have pictures."

She stood, ignoring Jack's warning look. "You better believe it. Right back." Charlotte made her way over the cream carpeted floor of the cozy living room to the wall of shelves. The room was bathed in gorgeous lamp and firelight, the gloomy day still not brightening outside. A large Christmas tree adorned in sparkling baubles and twinkling white lights added to the glow. We all had full bellies, Nigel having been persuaded to stay for an early lunch of shepherd's pie and red wine. Now we were drinking warm British tea again.

We were both exhausted, and the wine made me sleepier, but we were trying our best to stay occupied to avoid the jet lag that was sure to hit us.

"Mum," Jack groaned. He leaned back, his T-shirt stretching across his muscled chest, still looking indecently sexy. He desperately needed a shave, and I desperately needed to feel his stubble before he did so. Preferably on other parts of my body than just my hands. "Please stop, Mum. Keri Ann doesn't need to see my school play photos. Least of all when I was dressed as the pink snake in *Alice in Wonderland*."

"Oh, but I do." I snorted, overcome with the giggles again. I squeezed his hand where it sat on my thigh. "Did no one ever call them out for being overtly homo-erotic? I mean, pink worms? Seriously? I don't believe there are supposed to be pink worms in that book."

"Snakes," argued Jack. But his mouth couldn't contain his laughter either.

Personally, I wanted a shower. Our luggage had been delivered a few hours ago, and I was desperate to get out of these traveling clothes. "Snake, worm, whatever. And it was your acting debut… this I *have* to see." I looked over at Nigel.

His mouth had dropped open. "Blow me down," Nigel muttered. "You're right. Mr. Busby, the drama master, came out of the closet a few years after you left, mate. It was all the talk. To think? He was subtly trying to let everyone know even then. Making the boys prance about like little pink willies."

"I wouldn't call that subtle," said Jack and winked at me as we both cracked up.

"So you went to Jack's school too?" I asked Nigel.

He nodded. "A few years ahead of this guy, obviously. I'd left by the time he was there. But Mr. Busby taught me too. Saw him once several years later at a gay club in London." Nigel's eyes shifted to the left, and he suddenly flushed to the roots of his hair.

"Nooo," said Jack, incredulously. "You and Mr. Busby?"

"Stop it," Nigel snapped and glanced at Charlotte's back. He busied himself taking another sip of his tea. "Anyway, it was just the once," he added.

"Please tell me you were… of age?" I affected a dramatic whisper, emulating Jack's good-natured teasing.

Nigel grinned. "Well, I was, but I still called him *Mr. Busby*." He gave a little shoulder wiggle and twitched his eyebrow several times in a lascivious manner, joining in the fun.

"Eeeeeeew!" Jack howled. "Nige. Really?"

I let out a huge chuckle.

"Here they are," sang Charlotte as she plopped back on the chair on the other side of Jack and laid the photo album on the table.

"I can't believe we have to do a baby album on the first day," Jack groaned. "Surely we could've worked up to this."

"No way. This is fantastic."

The album had pictures ranging from Jack as a baby, through a toothy toddler, a gangly little boy, and then barely a picture of his teenage years, until his mom had started adding newspaper clippings of his early acting accomplishments. Charlotte turned the pages, slowly, almost to the end. "Well, after a while there were too many things to cut out and stick in here. My baby boy had made it." Although I had a feeling Charlotte had a box somewhere stuffed with all Jack's clippings, I couldn't imagine she'd let one pass her by.

Jack leaned over and gave his mother's shoulder a squeeze. She leaned into him.

"Oh, I worried so. Me being so far away and you being at the mercy of all those... vampires." She sniffed, then laughed at herself. "I'm so glad you came home. Both of you," she added to me.

"Thank you for making me feel welcome," I murmured, feeling a little overwhelmed. Jack turned his hand that was on my thigh palm up and squeezed my hand. "Looks like I should get some real pictures of you and Jack this Christmas, instead of newspaper clippings, so you can add to the album," I offered.

"Oh yes, that would be wonderful!"

Nigel stood. "All right, you lot. A man can't sit around on his arse all day. There's work to be done. I'm picking up some rich Russian footballer in a few hours. You've got my mobile, eh? Just gimme a shout when you need a ride."

"Yeah, man. Thanks." Jack stood too.

"I know you said you'd like to take Keri Ann to your friend Max's place down in Hastings for lunch one day. That still on?"

Jack shifted uneasily and glanced at me. "Um, I don't know. It might be a bit much if we're seen out."

"Oh," said Nigel. "Well, I can understand that. Max'll be disappointed though."

Did Jack feel like he couldn't do anything when I was with him because I was so leery of the press? I hated that for him. Like I was holding him back from going out and doing fun things. Especially seeing some old friends of his. But I couldn't deny I was nervous we'd blow our cover and our peaceful plans for Christmas would be shot. I resolved to bring it up with him later.

We all made our way back through the house to see Nigel off.

"You can always borrow mine or Jeff's car if you want to

go for a drive or something," Charlotte offered. "You don't have to wait on Nigel."

"Where is Jeff?" I asked. I'd heard a lot from Jack about the man who'd made Charlotte so happy.

"At work, I imagine," said Jack.

Charlotte nodded. "He's a solicitor. Works in the city still. Though I wish he'd cut back on his hours. He's up at five every morning to get the train in. But he gets home by six, so that's good."

We waved Nigel off, and then Jack grabbed our stuff that was still piled by the door. "Where are we sleeping?"

"Oh right, come on. You probably want to freshen up. Then Jack, you can take Keri Ann on a walk around the fields, show her the land. Maybe it will help give you guys a second wind so you can stay up until Jeff gets home."

"Sounds great. I'd love a hot shower," I said and literally felt Jack willing me to catch his eye. No freaking way. I didn't need to have hot naked showers in my head when I looked at him right now in front of his mother. My cheeks warmed as I flushed. It had to be so obvious that Jack and I were jonesing for some alone time. But, God, I didn't even know what the sleeping arrangements were. What if Charlotte wanted us in separate bedrooms? Surely she wouldn't.

four

CHARLOTTE TROTTED UP the wooden stairs, ahead of me. "Don't try these old stairs in socks. They're so smooth and worn with age, you'll go flying. I even slipped in shoes once. Anyway, maybe save your hot shower for after the walk, you'll probably want one later. Not sure how much capacity the old boiler has for multiple showers all day."

"I wish you'd—" Jack started.

"No more of that, Jack," Charlotte admonished.

I glanced back at him, my eyebrows raised. "Don't tell me. Jack wants to pay to replace your hot water heater," I stated as we followed.

He shrugged his shoulders, lips pursing as if to say, "And?"

Charlotte turned and rolled her eyes. "Of course he does.

And I keep telling him when the time comes, Jeff and I can handle it."

She showed us to a pretty floral bedroom with elegant green accents and botanical prints on the wall. There were two big windows with the same view as the kitchen, over the fields. "Uh, so um." She flushed, and my gut cinched tight with nerves. Dang, this was going to be worse than the birds and the bees talk my mom had tried when I was twelve. "You're adults and I'll leave you to make your own choices. This is what we call the Green Room. This bathroom here leads into the Blue Room, which is also made up. That's where Jack usually stays. But, uh, obviously, uh—"

"We'll be sharing, Mum," Jack said gently and set our bags down at the end of the large double bed. "Hope that's okay. And if it makes you feel uncomfortable, we can go to the hotel."

"Goodness, no, I'm fine. It's just, um, this is a first for me." She chuckled and walked over to an armoire in the corner and withdrew two fresh towels that she laid on the bed. "You've never brought a girl home, that's all, and I just didn't want Keri Ann thinking I was used to this sort of thing."

I let out a long slow breath. My belly flooded with churning nerves. I was embarrassed. But man was I happy to hear I was the only girl Jack had ever brought home. I mean, I had an inkling, based on how separate he liked to keep his lives and protect his mother from the craziness, but it was great to hear it anyway.

"But, um, I should just add that it's, um…" Okay now Charlotte was flushing again. This didn't bode well. What else was coming? "It's an old house, thin interior walls, sound carries," she rattled out, briskly. "Just so you know." She swallowed and cleared her throat as she headed toward the door.

I stood dumfounded. Too embarrassed to say a word.

Jack slapped his hand over his eyes, his shoulders shaking with laughter.

"So, anyway, that's it. See you downstairs in a bit, and I'll show you the best path to take on your walk. Cheerio," she added, slipping out the door.

"LOOK IN THE mirror." Jack stood behind me where I stood at the sink, having just brushed my teeth. I was wrapped in a towel, my skin chilled in the cool air. Having access to a hot shower had been too much to resist, and I'd rinsed my body quickly so as not to waste too much hot water. I'd twisted my hair up to keep it dry since we were going for a walk outside.

"I look tired," I responded, agreeing to his request by meeting his eyes in the mirror.

He leaned forward, placing his hands on the sink on either side of me. His hair was half sticking up and half flat. Hat hair. The dark stubble of his two-day-old growth made his green eyes stand out. Damn it, he was so sexy. "Yes, you do."

I elbowed him in the ribs.

"But you also look absolutely beautiful." He dropped his mouth to my bare shoulder and the curve of my neck, his unshaven face gently scraping. Eyes not breaking contact, his mouth opened, his teeth grazing, nipping my skin and his warm tongue soothing over me.

My belly flipped and swirled scalding liquid heat through my insides at the feel of him and sight of him behind me, the passion in his gaze. My breathing caught and went from slow and relaxed to shallow and choppy in an instant.

"I can't believe you snuck in here and got naked without me," he murmured against my skin, and his body pressed against my back.

Trying to turn to face him, I was stopped as he released one arm from the sink and wrapped it around my waist, holding me firm, my back to his front.

"Jack," I managed, swallowing my words as I felt his arousal.

He winked at me in the mirror.

"We, I, we're supposed to go downstairs. You heard your mom, we—" I broke off as his other hand left the sink and skated up my thigh and under the towel.

"God, I've missed you. So much." His head dropped to my shoulder and he inhaled deeply.

"I've missed you too." My voice was low and husky. I wanted nothing more than to be naked and wrapped up against Jack's hard and hot body, flesh to flesh, my heart beating as close to his as possible. "But we can't do this right now. It's, I—"

"I know, but let me just touch you. Please, I've been dying to." His hand made it around my hip, sliding across my lower belly, and skating downwards. His knee nudged my legs apart. I shuddered and he lifted his face, catching my eye again in the mirror.

"Jack."

"Shhhh." He drew the sound out softly. "You'll just have to be quiet. I'll be quick."

A knock sounded at the bedroom door, making me jump.

Jack straightened, leaving my skin bereft and tingling in his wake. Who was I kidding? More like aching and throbbing and... a belly as nauseous as if we'd been caught in the act.

"Jack, honey?" Charlotte's voice was hesitant.

He cleared his throat and winked at my mortified expression in the mirror before heading out of the bathroom.

I closed my eyes and released a breath. My point exactly. I finished getting dried off and putting on lotion as I listened to Jack answer the door to Charlotte. Apparently a bunch of packages had arrived for us.

Jack had told me to pack light because there was absolutely nothing in my wardrobe that could prepare me for a wet British winter. Having arrived and felt the icy, wet mist, that was almost a drizzle but not quite, I was inclined to agree. Especially now I'd seen that Charlotte practically lived in "wellies" as she called them. The closest thing I'd seen growing up in the Lowcountry were galoshes. Anyway, I knew they were available back home, but Jack had expressly told me not to bother with boots and rain jackets since they only made the best ones in England. Seemed like the stuff he'd ordered had arrived.

When the coast was clear, I came out of the bathroom.

Jack had opened most of the boxes but was hastily putting something away on top of the armoire. He turned and gave me a crooked smile.

"What was that?" I asked teasingly.

"One of your presents, so don't you dare look."

"Jack." My heart sank a little. "You're spoiling me. I can't do the same for you. I, I feel inadequate." It was true. I loved how excited he got when he gave me things, but I fought with myself and my reactions every time he did it.

"Keri Ann, you just being here with me is all I'll ever need. I know that sounds…" he cleared his throat and laughed lightly. "Yeah, it sounds freaking pathetic. I know."

"No, it doesn't," I whispered. "I can't think of anywhere I'd rather be than with you."

"But I know how hard it is for you with all the bullshit that follows me around."

"About that…" I perched on a tufted stool in front of a small antique vanity and faced him.

His eyes slipped to my legs and the towel that had ridden up. "Jack," I admonished with a ridiculous grin.

"Sorry."

"So, I was going to say, please don't feel like you can't go and see friends and stuff because of me, okay? I can handle a few photographers. I mean, I dread it, sure, but it's not the end of the world. And anyway, *you* could always go and I'll stay here and hang out with Charlotte. She was telling me we could drive down to the coast one day and go beach glass hunting."

Jack looked away, his mouth slipping into a frown.

"What?" I asked, confused by his reaction. "You don't think I'd like to spend time with your mom?"

He looked taken aback. "No, not that at all."

"What, then? My aversion to publicity? You already know that."

His hand raked through his unruly hair. "I don't know. Look, it's not that. It doesn't matter." He came around the bed in long strides and sat on the end of it in front of me.

It squeaked.

Awesome.

We both cringed. "You need to get some damn clothes on before I embarrass my mother. I'm getting to the point I might not care what sounds emanate from this bedroom."

He was deflecting from the issue at hand. The issue being more than just me not wanting to deal with a media frenzy. Something was weighing on his mind. I'd caught glimpses of it now and then. But what was it?

"It's called a stile." Jack stood by the wet mossy wooden contraption, holding out his hand in the cold, damp white-misted air. Did England, in fact, even have a sky? This was our second walk since our arrival yesterday, and I'd yet to see one.

I looked at his hand dubiously, then at the nonchalant looking bull in the distance behind his head while I breathed in the faint smell of cow dung and earthy wet stone. England. I kind of always thought it would feel, smell, and look like this. I loved it. It was so different from anything I'd grown up with.

"You just climb up on the board and swing your leg over the fence," Jack said patiently. He was wearing jeans, dark grey green wellington boots, "wellies," a dark green waxed *Barbour* rain jacket, and a tartan *Burberry* scarf wrapped around his neck. I didn't look much different. Although my "wellies" were dark brown as was my ladies' version of the jacket—the spoils of the many packages that had arrived. I felt like I was in a *Town & Country* photo spread.

"Are you sure we're allowed to?" I asked. "I mean why wouldn't they just put a gate in if they wanted people to pass."

"Well, they put the gates where it suits for farming, that doesn't always gel with where the footpaths are. A stile is just saying, look, I realize this is a public footpath that goes right through my land. You can go through it, but I don't have to like it."

"I'm sure they don't want anyone going through a field with a horny bull in it."

Jack chuckled at my expression and turned his dark head toward the creature in the distance. His hair ruffled in the arctic breeze, and the tips of his ears were tinged pink with cold. "He doesn't look horny."

"*You* don't look horny, but I bet I could get you there in two seconds flat."

Jack's raised his eyebrows, then dropped them, resigned. "That's a challenge I'll lose."

"Wait. So people can own land, but anyone has the right to walk through it?"

"Pretty much. If it has a Public Right of Way through it,

it's illegal not to allow access. Hurry up, are you going over or what?"

The bull snorted. It was staring at me.

Us.

No, me. Definitely me. "But they're letting us go into a field with a lone, irritated looking bull. And I'm wearing a red scarf!" A soft and luxurious scarf made of something called vicuña, courtesy of Jack's twelve days of Christmas, day six gift. I loved it. It was the softest thing, and probably the most expensive thing, I owned. "Is there a warning posted?"

"I guess it's the farmer's way of expressing his irritation at having to let people wander through. Keep us on edge a bit. I'm pretty sure they also have to legally post if it's a dangerous bull and not a juvenile. Or have a heifer in here with him to relieve him. Come on, already."

The bull resumed munching grass so I took Jack's hand and climbed up on the stile, swinging my leg over the fence, careful not to tear my jeans. I made it over and jumped down onto the thick, wet clumpy grass. Jack followed. The path, which was really more of a worn, flattened grassy line amongst the not so flattened grass, headed down a gently sloping hill along one side of the low stone wall and then curved to cut diagonally across a corner to another stile set midway through the far side. Infinitely closer to the bull.

"Relax," said Jack and cupped my cold cheeks with his gloved hands. His long lashes came to rest on his cheekbones as his face came down to meet my mouth with his. I tilted my face up, holding his wrists and welcomed his lips on mine.

His lips and nose were cold, but as his mouth opened, I drank in the heady heat of his tongue. Heat that poured down into me and pooled low.

"Mmm. You taste good," I murmured against his mouth. Sweet coffee and cinnamon. "Like Christmas."

He laughed. "Maybe that's your actual Christmas gift. Me, naked with just a red bow tied on my—"

"Jack!" I punched him on the shoulder, and we started walking down the hill. "What *would* your mother say?" But, too late I already had a vision of naked Jack in my head. "Anyway, I believe you already gave me that gift yesterday, your presence, remember?"

"But not my naked presence." With your cheeks red from the cold, I can't tell if you're blushing or not." He took my hand. "You're thinking about it, aren't you?"

"No."

"Yes, you are."

"No, I'm not." I grinned stupidly.

"Me. Naked. Go on, admit it."

"Actually, I was thinking of *me* naked, with just this delicate soft red scarf draped strategically—"

Jack growled and yanked me to a stop. His lips came down hard, his hot tongue sliding inside, and my body instantly went from a slow simmer to full roar. I found the stone wall at my back, and Jack pressed hard against me, one hand tangled in my hair and the other lifting my leg against his thigh. *Wow*.

He kissed desperately, and I matched him, my gloved hands grabbing on to him, trying to get closer. Impossible with all our layers. "God," Jack groaned, wrenching his mouth away like it was the hardest thing he'd ever done. "Do you realize how long it's been since I've been inside you?"

My stomach flipped as it always did when he spoke so plainly. I inhaled sharply as his hard thigh hit the right spot between my legs. Dull with all our clothes but perfect. Perfectly not enough. "Yeah," I gasped. "Three and a half weeks."

"Twenty six days. To be precise. Not that I'm counting. Except, yeah, I'm totally counting." His mouth nuzzled the spot under my ear, and my skin prickled.

"I'm so sorry I passed out last night." We'd had an early dinner, and I'd gone upstairs to get the hostess gift I'd brought for Charlotte and Jeff. I hadn't been able to resist stretching out on the bed for just a moment, and that was the last thing I remembered until I'd woken this morning wrapped in a cocoon of bedding. I was undressed to my underwear, but there was no sign of Jack. He'd gotten up early to spend some time with his mom.

"Well, surely you've, uh, relieved some of the pressure over the last—" The sight behind Jack stopped my words mid sentence. "Shit," I whispered in horror at the large black bull ambling in our direction over the deep green field. "Uh, Jack, it's a pretty big bull with rather large horns, and he's heading straight for us."

Jack turned his head, his body unmoving, just as the bull seemed to zone in on us and picked up his pace to a trot. I could see the condensation blowing from its nostrils. Or was it steam? Shit. I was frozen in panic. Any minute and it would stop, drop its head, and start pawing the ground ready to charge.

"Oh, fuck," said Jack.

five

JACK SPRANG INTO action. His hands went around my waist and lifted me up onto the wall and out of the way. The stones were cold and loose under my butt, and I wobbled.

"Quick, see if you can get down the other side," Jack said urgently. The bull snorted loudly.

I glanced behind me, a drop, but not terrible. "But what about you, can you climb up?" The bull slowed to a stop fifteen feet away, and we both froze. Its eyes were black and glossy, and it tilted its head up and to the side. "What's it doing?" I whispered. "Should we move or will it charge?"

"See if you can slowly slide off the other side. I'll edge back toward the stile."

"No, it's too far. Can you climb over the wall? It's loose though, be careful," I added as I dragged my legs over, dislodging a rock that went crashing off the side.

Just then the bull dropped its head. I scrambled over the other side, landing heavily, and turned back to see Jack leap up and get his torso over the wall that was almost as high as his chest. The bull charged, and I screamed. My chest caved, he wasn't going to make it. Without thinking, I ripped the scarf from around my neck, and waving it madly, ran down the hill along the wall. It was lower here, and in a stroke of luck, the bull was distracted for a second and turned toward me, stumbling with the abrupt move.

Jack scrambled over the wall, and found his feet, landing perfectly.

I dropped the scarf, and raced back up the hill toward him, launching myself into his arms.

"Ooof!" The muffled sound came out of Jack's mouth as my momentum tumbled us both down onto the wet ground.

I leaned up. "That's the last time I follow you blindly into a field." I smacked his arm.

"Ow." He laughed.

I slapped the top of his head.

He tangled his legs with mine, rolling me over onto my back and immobilized my wrists. "Wench."

"Idiot."

"Scaredy-cat."

"It was a fucking horny bull!" I squeaked.

"Ohh, dirty mouth. I love it." And his eyes zeroed in on the feature in question.

"You can at least thank me for saving your ass."

He raised his eyebrows. "I distinctly remember lifting you up out of harms way. I think I did the saving."

"I *literally* saved your ass. You would've had a horn up it if I hadn't waved my scarf around as a distraction."

Jack winced. "I guess it was lucky I gave you the scarf then. Again, *me* to the rescue."

"Ugh, you're impossible." But I was laughing at his ridiculousness.

"Impossibly turned on. I think it's officially becoming a dangerous condition."

"Certainly if it impairs your judgment and leads us into deadly situations."

"I'm thinking actually, more along the lines of those commercials where they tell you to seek medical help after four hours."

I giggled. "That's what I mean. The blood isn't circulating in your brain at all. Starved for oxygen, clearly. I'll have to take over all the decision-making from now on, or until we can find a way to remedy your malady."

"Funny girl. You're telling me you're just fine, huh?"

"Yep."

"Really?"

"Well, I managed twenty-one years without any at all, I'm

NATASHA BOYD & KATE ROTH

sure I'm still surviving after three and a half weeks."

"Twenty-six days," he corrected. "And what? I thought I was irresistible to you."

I flushed, the telltale heat warming my cold cheeks. Was I that easy to read? "You're heavy," I complained evasively.

Jack rolled off me, and I took a deep unconstricted breath. We could still hear the bull snorting on the other side of the wall. "Anyway, it was clearly *your* ass he was going for. Can't say I blame him," Jack said on an exhale.

"Is the sun finally burning off this mist, or am I imagining it?" I asked, squinting up into the whiteness above us. The earth was cold at my back but thankfully not seeping wetness through to my clothes thanks to my waxed jacket.

"We should be so lucky." Jack turned his head to look at me. "Apart from our near death experience, are you enjoying England?"

I smiled. "Yeah. It's exactly how I imagined it, actually. Which is a huge relief."

"So you're not missing being home? What's Joey decided to do for Christmas?"

"Dang, I was supposed to call him last night, and I forgot. I don't know yet. Last I heard he said he was going to stay at school and study. Which seems pretty bleak, but that's what he wanted. Will you remind me to call him when we get back to the house?"

"Sure. How's it going with Jazz? Have they still not sorted their shit out?"

"Jeez. One minute they're hot and heavy, and the next… well, let's just say my brother hasn't figured it out yet."

"What?"

"That she's his destiny. His homing beacon. The beach to his sea turtle." I cut my eyes over to him.

Jack rolled up onto an arm and looked down at me, black lashes framing his mesmerizing eyes. "Like you are to me." Then he put a gloved finger between his teeth and pulled his hand free. The hand went to the buttons of my jacket and undid them one by one.

I captured my bottom lip between my teeth as I waited to see what he was doing. Braced against the cold air, my insides swirled with heat. When his hand found the skin of my belly under my sweater, I jolted and stopped breathing. But he merely dragged his hand slowly upwards between my breasts until it was flattened palm down on my chest. There it stayed, my heart beating wildly against it like a bird in a cage.

"This. This right here, is my destiny. In here." He pressed down, his hand splayed on my breastbone as if imparting his emotions through his palm, willing me to feel something more than he was saying. "You're the beach to my sea turtle." He gave a lopsided grin, his dimple showing up. "My homing beacon. Actually, just… you're my home. You're where my heart lives."

I released a long sigh. "Jack."

He leaned down and kissed me gently, briefly, then raised his head again, his eyes burning into me. "There's something I wanted to talk to you about. I was going to wait, but…" he trailed off, his brow furrowing like he wasn't sure he should have said anything. Light began warring with clouds in his eyes.

Wait to talk to me about something? Why? Maybe I wouldn't like what it was about… or maybe he was going to wait for a special day, like Christmas. What would he talk to me about on Christmas that he couldn't talk about any day? Unless it was something special. Like… worry hurtled through my body. My jaw locked and my chest seized. My eyes widened. I wasn't ready to talk about settling down or getting married. What did that even look like with our crazy schedules? It was a recipe for us to try and fail and possibly fracture apart forever.

"Don't," I rushed out.

"Don't what?" he asked, taken aback by my abrupt interruption.

I swallowed the weird ball of panic that was suddenly clogging my throat. *Don't panic, don't panic. You don't even know what he was going to say.*

Jack's eyes were creased in confusion, and then hurt seemed to fill his face. "What did you think I was going to say?" he whispered. His lips looked pale.

"Nothing, I don't know." I swallowed again, since the damn thing in my throat was still there, now filled with guilt. And I *didn't* know what he was going to say. No, not at all. "I just… you didn't seem sure you wanted to talk about it, whatever it is. So don't." I was babbling awkwardly.

"Bullshit," Jack said. His hand slipped out from under my sweater, leaving me chilled, and sat up. Resting his arms on his knees, he looked off over the green fields and into the white-coated distance.

I sat up and drew my coat back around me. "I'm sorry," I said. "I panicked."

"I gathered that. The question is 'about what'?"

"I—nothing."

"Hence the reason I called bullshit," Jack said with a weary sigh. He pulled a tuft of grass free and threw it. "Aren't couples supposed to be able talk to each other?"

"You're one to talk. You've had something bothering you ever since you met me from L.A. Even before that, I could tell on the phone. And you haven't talked about it at all."

"Well, maybe that was what I was going to talk to you about just then," he said. But he didn't sound convincing.

"Bullshit," I whispered, and hated that I said it. He'd made a good point after all, if he *was* going to tell me, I was the one who'd cut him off.

He turned his head to look at me and gave a slight shrug. "It was a part of it."

"Oh."

Jack got to his feet and dusted the wet grass off his jeans, then pulled his glove back on. He reached out a hand to help me up, and I gratefully accepted.

As I brushed the wet grass and dirt from my own outfit, Jack retrieved my scarf from the ground down the hill. It was damp and probably ruined.

"Come on, let's head back before we catch colds," Jack said absently and set off along the wall back to the footpath, my red scarf tucked under his arm. I did my buttons up hastily and then folded my arms across my chest, hugging myself tightly, and followed. After a few minutes where I tried to keep up and not feel hurt he was marching off without me, he stopped and held out his hand. I ran, wellies sliding on wet grass, and grabbed it. He shook his head with a small smile, and we kept walking. Sometime soon, Jack and I were going to have to get really intimate. And by that I meant we were going to have to have some really honest and vulnerable conversations about our future.

"So, Jeff's awesome," I said as we walked, choosing a neutral topic of conversation for now.

"He is, isn't he? It's clear my mom and he have a great relationship. He adores her."

"That must be a huge comfort to you, living so far away."

"Yeah, it is. I wish he'd retire, though; he works too hard. Spend some more time with my mum. She's happy, but I get the sense she's a tad lonely out here all by herself."

"Really? I don't know her that well, but I think she enjoys the solitude."

"You might be right."

"So is Charlotte her real name?"

Jack pursed his lips. "Sure is."

"But yet, everyone calls you Jack? And not William?"

"I've been Jack since I was nine years old."

"But isn't—"

"That's who I am Keri Ann," Jack snapped, stopping and letting go of my hand. "Jack-freaking-Eversea, remember?"

"Don't speak to me that way, Jack. And how could I *freaking* forget?" I mimicked.

"Dammit. Sorry." He turned to me and stuffed his hands in his pockets, blowing out a misty cloud of condensed breath. His nose was red from cold, his cheeks ruddy, but he still was the most beautiful man in the world. And something was bothering him. I hated to think it had been me who upset his carefully balanced mood. I knew he disliked being back in England, his mother notwithstanding. He started to say something, then stopped, and mashed his lips together.

I didn't know what was coming, but I felt like we'd probably have a better time to talk about serious stuff when we were warm and dry, and in a better place than this odd edgy moment we were having. "So, not sure how you feel about this, but you've been sliding into a British accent."

His eyes widened in surprise as his head drew back abruptly. "No, I haven't."

"Yeah." I laughed. "You have. You're all… 'bloody hell,' and 'spot of tea,'" I mimicked in a overdramatic way, dropping down several octaves.

"Oh, man. You shouldn't try an English accent." Jack laughed. He walked up to me and wrapped me up in his arms. "I love you so much."

I loved him back. So much. And the depth of my feelings stole the smile off my face. "I love you too, Jack."

Those words seemed inadequate.

"Say it again," he said in a low voice.

I took a deep breath. "I love you."

As I stared up into his eyes, I wondered if Jack thought love was enough.

six

WE WERE COLD and quiet by the time we had trudged all the way back to The Grange. Charlotte was in the kitchen with an older lady with white hair, wedged in at the table holding a mug of tea with both hands. The older lady's round face creased into a huge smile as we walked in, and she pushed her chair back to stand up.

"There you are." Charlotte beamed just as Jack made a sound of surprise and hurried forward to practically lift the older lady out of the chair.

"Mrs. Eversea, I can't believe it's you. You never age a bit. What's your secret?" Jack gushed.

She gave him a squeeze. "Oh tosh! You charmer, you." But she laughed delightedly.

I was so happy when Jack told me he'd gotten

reacquainted with Mrs. Eversea the last time he was in England.

Jack grinned. "Saw Nigel, he's looking well."

"So I heard. You're a sweetheart for giving him the work." She set him at arm's length, inspecting him head to foot.

"Of course," he assured her. "Though, I think he helps me out more than the other way around."

Mrs. Eversea clucked and looked past Jack to catch my eye. I suddenly realized I was more nervous about meeting this lady who'd saved Jack's life once upon a time than I was his mother. "So," she said seriously and looked between Jack and me as he stepped to the side, putting a hand on my elbow about to introduce me. "This is the girl you're going to marry?"

There was an instant of silence and the loud clattering of a spoon Charlotte was holding.

My heart seemed to stop and give one long, loud, thud.

And then Jack let out a sound. A cross between a breath and a laugh. Strangled and torturous.

A sound that gouged meat hooks into my heart. Painful.

"Oh, one day," said Charlotte, casually picking up the spoon. "They're still young. Keri Ann still has college."

Charlotte. I could kiss her. But had Jacked talked to her about it? Had she talked him out of it? Into it? If indeed that was what he was planning. Aaaah, God, my head was reeling, my heart thudding.

Jack still hadn't said anything.

Jack, still hadn't said anything.

Shit, this was my queue.

Since Jack was still standing in the minefield afraid to move, I stepped forward. "Nice to meet you, Mrs. Eversea. I'm Keri Ann Butler. Jack's told me so much about you."

"Ha! That accent! I could listen to you all day. Come here," she said and pulled me into a hug that smelled of violets and laundry detergent. "You're a brave girl putting up with his shenanigans." She released me. "Don't know how you do it. All those blasted photographers. Absolute vultures, the lot of them." She huffed and backed up her larger frame into the kitchen chair. "Don't you dare let him tie you down 'til you're good and ready. Give the boy a chance to get his life a bit steadier too."

Charlotte set two steaming mugs on the table. "Here's some tea for you both, you look frozen to the bone."

"Thanks," Jack said and pulled out two chairs for us.

"Uh, do you mind if I take my tea upstairs? I need to call my brother and let him know I made it here safely."

Jack aborted his movement to sit down. "I'll come up and get you my phone."

"That's okay. You stay and catch up." I kissed him on the cheek and gave everyone a cheerful smile. "I can manage."

Jack nodded and sat. He added milk and two spoons of honey to my tea and handed it to me. "We had a 'run in' with a bull," he said to Charlotte and Mrs. Eversea and launched into our story as I quietly went upstairs. I would have actually liked to stay and be a part of that, but the need to be alone for a moment to clear my head was too overwhelming.

That's exactly what I was. Overwhelmed. I hadn't realized how much until right in that moment in the kitchen. I'd felt the full weight of the love his family had for him and the nervousness I felt about being accepted by them. And of course, the unspoken issue of our future. Jack was done filming in Savannah. He'd stayed as long as possible but had been back in Los Angeles doing post-production and voiceover work for sound issues. Soon, he would be on a publicity tour for the movie, and he was already in the planning stages of another movie he was scheduled to be in, shooting down in Uruguay. I'd been putting all of this out of my head, just making it through to the end of the semester and looking forward to having Jack all to myself for three weeks over Christmas break.

But I didn't have him to myself, not really. It wasn't just being here with his mother and Jeff and Mrs. Eversea. It was all the other weirdness Jack seemed to carry around with him here.

I grabbed Jack's phone off the dresser and sat on the end of the squeaky bed to dial my brother's number.

IT WAS LATE, and I lay awake in the large cold bed alone. Apparently, Jack had left in Charlotte's car sometime during my phone conversation with Joey and still wasn't home. I'd stayed up as late as possible with Charlotte and Jeff. Jeff was charming and gruff, a handsome man with silver hair and friendly blue eyes. We'd had dinner and played scrabble but time ticked on. I was worried sick, as we all were, especially as he didn't have his phone. Charlotte asked me twice if Jack and I were okay. Which was acutely embarrassing, despite the fact I knew she only meant it in the way of a concerned mother whose son has run off and she wants to make it right.

Finally, Nigel called and told us that Jack had called him from Hastings. He'd had too much to drink and couldn't drive Charlotte's car home and had asked Nigel to go and get him. It was over an hour's drive away.

Concern gave way to anger and simmered away inside me.

I heard the sound of a car on the gravel sometime after midnight. The dull thud of the front door. The murmuring voice of Jeff, clearly upset we'd had to get ourselves so worried. The trudge of a heavy booted foot up the creaking stairs and hallway to our bedroom. And past our bedroom toward the Blue Room. Was he fucking serious, right now?

I slapped back the covers and ran straight to the bathroom and through it to the door on the other side, wrenching it open. I stood, my chest heaving as Jack froze halfway in from the hall.

The Blue Room was smaller than ours by far and had a single bed coming out from one wall, and an armchair in the other. Jack dominated the space.

He squeezed his eyes shut at the sight of me and pressed the door closed behind him, sealing us in.

I could smell the whisky across the ten feet separating us.

"Not tonight, please," he muttered, slurring. He was still in his jeans and shirt he'd worn earlier and a pair of heavy, undone lace up boots. "You're mad. You have every right to be mad. I didn't want to wake you and have you be... more mad." He swayed, and I unfolded my arms on a sigh and stepped toward him.

"I'm fine." He staggered back from me.

"Jack, just let me help you. Okay?"

"I'm fine," he said again and stumbled toward the bed where he fell face down, his feet off the end.

I stood still a moment, the energy behind my anger completely gone. Then I went down on my knees to loosen his boots and pull them and his socks off. I took a moment to press a kiss to my fingertips and transfer it briefly on the small sea turtle that was inked into the skin of his foot. Jack stirred and turned his head, his eyes finding mine and watching me.

"I'm sorry," he said, his voice muffled. Then he closed his eyes.

Standing, I grabbed a blanket that was draped over the corner armchair and laid it over his body. His breathing was already deep and even. He'd need water.

I went back to our bedroom, pulled my shoes on, and headed downstairs in my flannel pajama pants and long sleeved Henley.

Charlotte and Jeff were at the kitchen table, talking in low voices. I stopped, uncomfortable. "Sorry, I was just going to get Jack some water."

She smiled at me in welcome, and Jeff cleared his throat and got up. "I'm heading to bed. Early start again." He leaned down and kissed Charlotte's forehead. "I'll be glad come the weekend, then a nice break for Christmas. Good night, Keri Ann," he said as he went past me.

I walked to the table and sat down. "Does he always act like this when he's here?" I asked. "Disappearing off and coming home drunk?"

Charlotte sighed. "I was going to ask you the same thing."

"Not really. Not since we've been together anyway." I twisted my fingers. "He says he finds it hard to be here, in England. Maybe that's what it is."

"Maybe. I also think he's feeling insecure."

"About what?"

"You, I would imagine."

"Me?" I asked, taken aback. "Why?"

"Honey, I've never seen Jack in love before. There was this girl in New York, when we lived there, a silly teenage crush. Not that there weren't other girls, mind you. But it's the only other time in his life I've seen him close."

Sharp jealousy pricked at me.

Charlotte fiddled with the edge of a placemat still on the table. "But of course, he was young and she barely acknowledged his presence," she was quick to add. "He's never given his heart away easily. He's always been closed up so tight; I wondered how on earth he'd survive in Hollywood. It still baffles me. But I've come to realize he literally has two personalities. One he's created, and the one he is inside. I worry that his outside one has reinforced the feeling he doesn't believe he has much to offer anyone beyond glitz and glamour." She took a sip from her mug.

I sat still, hanging on her every word.

"I'm sure that's one of the reasons you and he work so well together. That's the one part you have zero interest in. But I'm wondering if perhaps that could also be part of the problem."

My brow furrowed. "What do you mean?"

"Just that you've given him direction and meaning and become such a large part of his life I think it's made that other part of him even emptier. Made him aware of what it would mean for him if you suddenly weren't there for some reason. If he... lost you. I think it terrifies him."

My heart squeezed. I thought of how I shut down conversations about our future all the times he brought them up. Not because I didn't want a future with him, but because I felt if we fixed our future too tight, it was more likely to break. We needed wiggle room. Flexibility to grow and change together. I just wanted to take things a step at a time. Make sure I wasn't losing myself and my dreams along the way. "I get scared when he brings up our future," I admitted. "You said it yourself, I'm still young. I still haven't figured out my dreams, beyond my art and finishing school. I'm scared I'll wake up in a few years and be in this life he created for us and have had no hand in what it looks like. I want to make sure we are living and growing together, shaping our dreams together. And he needs to be in California for his career and..." I swallowed as I geared up to admit the truth out loud. "I hate it there, Charlotte. I hate who he is there. I can't stand seeing him don that weird empty facade and pretend he likes half the people I know he hates. I don't ever want to live there." There, I'd said it. God, I was so selfish. I just wanted Jack to fit into *my* life and not fit into his. My eyes burned with the urge to make tears.

Charlotte squeezed my hand. "So you don't really accept that part of his life?"

"I'm never going to relish getting spied on and misquoted. Let alone, get over the insecurity I feel every time I go out with people, wondering if I'm good enough for him. But I do accept that part of his life, or I wouldn't be here with him. I haven't done a very good job of proving that though, have I?"

"Maybe he does need to know you can exist in both of his worlds. And you know what? You *are* young, but your words tell me you are probably a lot wiser than your years. I feel sure you two will get it worked out."

I sniffed and nodded. "Thank you."

She smiled and patted my hand.

"So what's in Hastings?" I asked. "Is that where his friend from school lives who Nigel mentioned?"

"Yes. Max. I didn't realize they'd gotten back in touch, but I for one am happy to see him reintegrate parts of his old life with his new life. He'd cut all ties, you know? Refused to even acknowledge his childhood here. Max is a good sport, owns an old house by the fishing docks in Hastings that he's turned into a successful restaurant and inn."

"So them getting back in touch won't blow Jack's identity then? Aren't you worried they'll come and harass you?"

She laughed. "I'm sure people would care for about a split second, but then who's going to give a toss what some over-the-hill lady like me is doing down here in the middle of the countryside on a daily basis? I think Jack cares more than I do, frankly. But anyway, it's been wonderful in the sense that he has this safe place to come to where no one would ever think to look. That would be gone. I think that's why we've all worked hard to keep it hidden so long. But anyway, Max is a good chap. I can't imagine him ever telling anyone Jack's real name. They'll just think he had a celebrity friend. That's all."

I failed to hold in a huge yawn.

"Oh me too, look at the time." Charlotte glanced at the delicate antique-looking watch on her wrist. "Jeff and I are going up to London tomorrow, together. I need to do some last minute shopping, and we're due for dinner with friends. We'll be back the following morning. Is that all right? Will you two be all right here for meals and what not?"

Alone.

With Jack.

For twenty-four hours.

I could have kissed her. As it was, I hugged her good night and took a glass of water for Jack. Tomorrow I needed to sort things out between us, lay some of Jack's fears to rest, and get naked with him as soon as possible.

seven

SLIPPING INTO THE darkened room, I left the door to the lighted bathroom open so I could see where I was going with Jack's water. It was a good thing I was wide awake on American time because I had a lot to figure out in my head.

We were three days into our three weeks together, including travel time, and things weren't going the way I'd imagined. We'd been desperate for this time together. The last few months had consisted of intense moments stolen from our otherwise single and busy lives, him with work, me with school. The few weekends we'd managed were focused and protected from the outside world by going to extraordinary lengths, and we'd never addressed anything beyond our happiness to be together. The island of Daufuskie near my hometown resort of Butler Cove had been a destination more than a few times due to its difficult access. And Jack didn't have a problem flying. Perhaps we'd put too much pressure on ourselves. Jack had gone running from us today, but I wasn't necessarily mad. I recognized my own culpability in the situation.

In the early days I'd had to watch as each new week brought another random woman from the pages of media sensationalism, claiming to have had a piece of the cheating Jack Eversea. Mostly, we'd tried to avoid seeing any media, but it was almost impossible. Jack's reputation as a cold and careless Lothario grew stronger with each publication, and our spirits had dimmed in response. Trying to believe it was all lies had put my heart and my pride through an unimaginable house of horrors last summer. But seeing how each new article hurt Jack had definitely solidified the fact we were in it *together*. I thought we'd grown stronger since then, but perhaps we really hadn't. Perhaps, *I* hadn't.

I set the water down gently, so caught up in my thoughts, I jumped as a warm rough hand clasped mine.

Jack was watching me from where he lay the same way I'd left him. Face down but with his head turned to the side. Light from the bathroom sliced across his face, illuminating his glassy green eyes and dark stubbled jaw. His soft brown hair glinted, and I itched to slide my fingers through it.

"You scared me." I breathed out a small laugh. "I brought you some water."

He blinked slowly, and his hand squeezed mine gently. "I often wonder," he whispered so softly I leaned closer to hear, "what would have happened if Audrey's story had come out before you decided we were worth a shot."

I swallowed, heavily. "What do you mean?" Audrey's story of Jack cheating on her with me, as well as countless other women, had hurt. Despite it all being lies, she'd won the sympathy of celebrity gossips everywhere when she claimed the stress of it had made her lose their baby.

"I mean... I don't think we'd be together."

"Jack," I said, my voice catching. "What are you saying?" I sank to my knees on the floor by his bed, close to his head.

"Not on my part, baby, don't worry."

"So on *my* part then?" I asked.

He didn't respond, just watched me in the darkened room, his gaze heavy on my heart.

I shifted toward him more and pressed my hand against his back, the warmth of his body seeping through his shirt, trying to understand where this was coming from. Then I gave in to the need to slide my fingers through his silky hair. "Jack?" My voice was confused and thready.

He closed his eyes in a long blink. "I often thank my lucky stars you are so good at doing things you set out to do," he said quietly, opening his eyes again. They were deep and shining and settled on me. "Determined to stick by your decisions. I'm always grateful you picked us before the shit hit the fan. I'm not sure you would have if the shit had hit first."

A huge lump materialized in my esophagus. I drew my hand from his hair, confused by what he was saying or why. Thinking back on that time was hard. We'd gone through so much. But I knew in my heart, I would have always picked Jack. He knew it too. Surely.

"You're drunk, Jack." I shook my head.

"Would you have?" he pressed, his eyes suddenly revealing his vulnerability.

My heart heaved. How long had he been feeling this? Had I just not seen it?

"Would you have fought for me?" he asked.

I thought back to the moments when I'd let doubt creep in, even before the scandal had thrown our lives upside down. I knew my indecisiveness about giving Jack another shot hadn't made for the most convincing case, but what did he expect? Of course I'd needed time to get my head and my heart aligned. Life wasn't a movie script where someone said the one magic word or phrase that erased all doubt and misconception and suddenly everyone understood and all was forgiven. We'd gone through this. I thought we'd moved past it.

"Do you even want to be with me? Or will it cause too much publicity to break it off?"

I inhaled sharply. Knowing he was coming from a

vulnerable and scared place took the edge off, but it still stung.

"Never mind. Don't answer that." Jack breathed out and rolled onto his back. He brought his hands up and tucked them under his head, his soft T-shirt stretching over his chest and rising up to reveal a strip of taut abdomen.

"I'm not sure how I'm supposed to answer," I tried, keeping my voice steady. "I think you're asking me whether I truly love you and want to be with you or if I'm just sticking with you to prove to the world I wasn't one of your bimbos. And frankly I'm not sure what that says about how you think of me." I folded my arms, protecting my heart. "Of us."

Shit, did he bring me all the way to England to break up with me? *Okay, head case Keri Ann. Seriously?* I tried to take a deep breath, but it caught as my chest seized. My eyes and nose prickled to hold in the agonizing possibility. Damn it. I blew out a breath. And tried to get on an even keel with him. "You know the answer to that, Jack. You know I picked you and would do it again, and again, in a thousand different ways. I love you. I do fight for you. Everyday that I don't let malicious gossip slip through my trust in you. My belief in you. In us. Everyday that I live this life with you and let myself believe you picked this normal, boring small-town girl instead of a thousand willing beauty queens—" My voice caught, and I stood up, mad that I'd let his drunken ramblings upset me. I should have just let him sleep it off. *But he is telling you his truth without any inhibitions. This is what has been on his mind.* My inner voice was a real pain in the ass.

His hand reached out and grabbed mine again, and he used it to half pull himself up to sitting, swinging his legs off the bed. His upper body swayed a moment, and then he brought his forehead down to rest low on my waist, his arms wrapping around me, pulling me to stand between his thighs. "Jesus, baby. I'm sorry. I drank too much." He exhaled, his breath hot against my belly. "I could stand in front of a thousand women who people tell me are the most beautiful, the most sexy, and you are still the most stunning woman in the world. You're the *only* woman in the world. The only girl I see." His face tilted up toward me. "Who I will *ever* see."

I sank my hands into his hair, holding his head. "You're the only one I see too."

His face eased against my abdomen, his cheek nudging my top until I felt his stubble against my stomach. His warm mouth followed, sending shivers over my skin in the chilled room. "And though you're far from boring... or normal," he added with a slight slur and a chuckle, "the description— normal boring small-town girl is the description of my dream girl. Then you add this soft skin..." His mouth moved over my belly and his hand closed in a firm grip on one of my pajama-bottom-clad butt cheeks. "And this incredible ass..."

"Jack!" I squeaked, conscious of our conversation carrying.

He looked up. His eyes weren't quite focused. "And that freaking unbelievably beautiful face. Those eyes that tell me so much with no words. Those sexy freckles…"

"I don't have freckles."

"Faint, sure. But you do, across your nose and upper cheeks."

I pursed my lips.

Jack didn't finish his train of thought but rested his forehead on my belly again, and his hands tightened on my pajama pants at the side of my hips and pulled down gently.

"What are you doing, Jack?" I whispered and went to still his hands.

"Let go, Keri Ann."

Something in his voice and his breathing made me comply, and I stood still as his hands pushed my pajama pants down my thighs, and then, after a sharp inhale by Jack as he took in my lack of underwear, down to the floor.

The cool air of the room prickled at the skin on my legs. "Step out of them."

I hesitated less than a second, and then toed my shoes off to the sound of a light chuckle from Jack. The return trip of his warm hands up my newly bared skin was hot and branding.

My breathing stuttered. "J-Jack."

"Shh," he breathed, his mouth moving in hot kisses down my belly. "I want to taste you."

Oh. Holy shit.

My legs wobbled as my knees tried to hold the weight of heavy pulsing lust that had just broken the dam of pent-up longing I'd been so carefully handling. My hands shook, and I slid them into his hair.

"God, I love that sound you make."

"What sound?"

I made a sound?

Jack's warm, rough hand made contact with my inner thigh and immediately glided upwards. "Open your legs wider."

I bit down on a whimper gasp thing. His buzzed state was certainly making him wordy. Bossy. Not that he wasn't usually.

"*That* sound," he said on a soft chuckle. His eyes were glassy but now focused.

God, I was already making noise, and he hadn't done anything yet. We really should stop. We had the whole day tomorrow. Besides, after the amount Jack had probably had to drink. "Jack, I'm not sure you're in any fit state to—"

His fingers found my slick flesh, already primed for him. *Traitorous body.*

I gasped.

"Ah, fuck, Keri Ann." His curse, his voice, rough and low and laden with need, was as potent as the searing arousal caused by his moving fingers. They slid over me, teasing me, asking me, and then starting a slow and torturous rhythm.

Mashing my lips together, in order to seal my mouth closed, I tried to control my response. It was no use. "Jack," I burst out, my body trembling.

"Baby," he groaned, his eyes not leaving my face. The other hand gripping my hip moved up my chest, pausing a moment to scrape over the tip of my breast through my cotton top before moving up to my neck and my jaw.

Shuddering, I closed my eyes on a sigh, heightening the feel of his fingers moving and sliding between my legs, focusing. Circling. My hips responded of their own accord.

"Does it feel good?" he whispered.

I nodded against his hand on my cheek, my pulse pounding, my chest rapidly expanding and contracting.

"Tell me," he said, and his fingertips on my face moved over my mouth coaxing it open.

"It feels a—amazing," I stuttered.

Jack's fingers between my legs slid back, and then forward… and then deep inside me.

"Oh my—Aaah—"

My desperate sound was abruptly muted down to a long whimper as the fingers at my jawline slid into my mouth. I quaked, my body rocking forward, driving him deeper between my legs, completely out of my control.

"Shit," he muttered.

I sucked at the fingers in my mouth, desperately trying

not to let a sound escape me. All it did was intensify every pull and glide of his hand as his fingers moved in and out of my aching body.

"Shit, Keri Ann. Baby." Jack's voice was strangled and not that quiet. Hearing himself must have shocked him because suddenly he withdrew his hands.

"Please, don't... don't stop."

In a moment, he'd stood, flipped our positions and had me lying on the bed. He dropped to his knees on the floor between my legs.

Oh, God.

I caught his dark gaze.

Both of us were breathing heavily. I felt so desperate. So uninhibited all of a sudden. I needed this. I needed Jack. These times, these raw, sensual times between us, when our words and our responses were the most honest, seemed to strip our souls bare to each other, reminding us that "us together" was more important than all the other *BS* we let dictate our moods and feelings.

"I'm so far from stopping," he smirked, his eyes glinting at me before his gaze dropped between us. "I've missed you so much." His fingers that had been inside me went to his mouth.

"God, Jack," I rasped. How did he do this to me? Nothing was shocking with Jack, it was all natural and painfully arousing.

He pressed two fingers to my entrance, and I found myself rocking against them, my body desperate for relief, for friction.

"Please."

A low throaty chuckle sounded as Jack moved his head closer. "What do you want, Keri Ann?" he whispered.

Self-consciousness began to squeeze my stomach, creeping into my mind. His breath was so close to where I needed him, it was making me desperate and nervous, my body clenching with tension. "You know what I want."

"I want you to ask me." There was no teasing in his voice, just pure need.

"You. I want you, your mouth, your hands; I don't care. I need you. Please." My voice broke.

"God, I love hearing that, you have no idea." The last word was a mumble as his mouth made contact, his hot tongue flicking over me. His fingers thrust deep inside, forcing a sharp exhale out of my chest, relief and the sting of need all jumbled together. He withdrew and began to pump in a slow sensual rhythm.

Churning, dizzying heat twisted my stomach and poured through my veins. My hands grabbed at Jack's hair, the sheets, and eventually, and more usefully, the pillow. I held back, attempting to keep my responses in check, in silence, gritting my teeth, and steeling my body. With the need to be quiet, I was pressure-filled and only getting wound tighter. And then I was past the point of no return, and yet it was still building.

Jack was relentless and focused, his tongue and his hands clearly not at all impinged by the alcohol he'd obviously consumed.

I was coming apart. I was hurtling down a track as bolts and ties tore loose inside me, but I couldn't let go. Or maybe I simply couldn't stop. I bucked against Jack's mouth.

His free hand held me down, his fingers biting into my thigh, an answering groan seemed torn from his throat, vibrating against me.

"I can't..." I tried. But then I did. My eyes screwed shut, squeezing desperate tears that came out of nowhere. I arched wildly against his mouth, forcing him harder against me. My climax roared through me, and forcing the pillow into my open mouth, I screamed silently.

A desperate sound came from Jack, and I was suddenly being pulled forward off the bed and onto his thighs. His mouth found mine, and I tasted myself mixed with a smoky whisky on his tongue as he kissed me deeply, his arms like steel bands around my body.

eight

JACK WAS HUNG over.

And I needed to get him back to optimum performance as soon as possible. I had eggs and bacon made, black coffee and orange juice standing by, and Paracetamol, which Charlotte had assured me was the same as Tylenol, lying in wait. Nigel was arriving in an hour to take us to Max's place for lunch and to get Charlotte's car that Jack had abandoned. Charlotte and Jeff had left at the crack of dawn.

I opened with the juice and a painkiller. "Wakey, wakey, rise and shine," I sang, standing over the lump in the bed. His head was wedged under a pillow, and he emitted a long groan. "I have something you want," I added.

"Does it include you, naked?" his gruff, disembodied voice asked.

"Uh, no."

"Then I don't want it."

"It's better than that," I assured him.

He flung the pillow off his head, revealing a scowl and hair all over the place. He squinted up at me. "There's nothing better than that."

"There's a painkiller. So you might actually enjoy it if I take my clothes off."

He looked at me a beat longer, then held out his hand.

I plopped the pills into his palm and held out the juice while he scooted up onto an elbow.

"Why are you so chipper?" he asked. "Aren't you supposed to be mad at me or something?"

"Is that what you were trying to accomplish?"

"No. I was being an asshole. I'm sorry. I shouldn't have gone off like that without telling you where I was going."

"Or taking your mom's car so she had to get up at five this morning to go into the city with Jeff."

"Shit. Are you serious? Oh my God." He dropped his head into his hands.

"I'm kidding. She is gone, but only because she planned to do that anyway. You need to get your ass out of bed so we can go get her car. Nigel will be here soon."

"You *are* mad at me."

"Nope. I'm not. Not after what you accomplished last night. My feelings got hurt, and I was worried about you. We all were. Now get up, but take a shower first, you smell like an old pub."

"Um… when you say what I accomplished last night, are you referring to the shattering orgasm I gave you? Because I feel like that should be a free pass for any future bullshit too."

"I can't believe you even remember it, to be honest. I think you were pretty tanked."

"Baby, that was so intense, I practically came just getting you off. I probably would have, if I'd been sober. Trust me, I'm not likely to forget that in a hurry."

"As amazing as it was—"

"As incredible, no, mind-blowing… as *mind-blowing* as it was," he modified my sentence, "… continue."

I picked up a small toss pillow and threw it at him.

He caught it midair.

"As *mind-blowing* as it was," I conceded. "It is definitely not a free pass for future bullshit."

His mouth quirked in a sexy grin. "Seriously? I'll have to try harder next time."

"I guess you will." I widened my eyes and shrugged, pretending nonchalance. "Now, come on."

He let out a deep laugh and dropped his head back on the bed. "You don't need to come with me to get the car. I can be back in a couple of hours."

"Well, I want to meet Max, so I guess you'll have to endure my company. We're having lunch with him."

"You do? We are?" A large smile spread across his unfairly handsome hungover face as he propped himself back up. "But that'll be like..." His eyes widened dramatically. "*In public,*" he whispered.

"*I know.*" I smirked. "See you downstairs."

"Wait," he said and sat up abruptly, then winced and grabbed his head. "Damn."

"What?"

"Damn it. We are finally alone in the house together and there's not a chance I could lure you into this bed with me is there?" He reached for another sip of juice.

"Answer me this. Does your alcohol pickled mouth feel like the bottom of Gandhi's flip flop?"

Jack snorted and choked on his juice.

I walked over and thumped his muscly back, shaking my head in mock pity. "Well, there's not a chance I'm kissing it."

"You mean-spirited hoyden," Jack griped.

THE DRIVE DOWN to Hastings took a little over an hour. Jack with a full belly and some painkillers was feeling better, and the two of us lounged in the back, me leaning against him, my back held tightly to his chest in a comfortable embrace. I wanted to watch the scenery but we both ended up dozing.

It was cold and clear down at the coast.

"The town is technically St. Leonards-on-Sea. On really clear days, you're supposed to be able to see France," Jack murmured, following my gaze out the window as we arrived. The sky reflected blue flakes twinkling across the water. Upon closer inspection, after Nigel let us out by the sea wall, the English Channel was as brown and churned up as the ocean in my part of the world. But there were no marshes here. Just rocks, pebble beaches, and a shit load of seagulls perched on pier pilings. In the distance was a fleet of brightly painted fishing boats. It was bracingly cold, the wind off the water whipping my hair across my cheeks.

I turned away from the water and the wind. The town was nestled in by sheer cliff faces. The road along the sea wall was lined with lampposts wrapped in Christmas greenery and lights that were probably beautiful at night.

Max's place opposite us was a renovated Victorian townhome, painted pale grey and retrofitted with huge windows. It was beautiful. The sea views must be stunning from inside. Jack had explained that far from an inn, it was more of a luxury boutique hotel. There were hardly any pedestrians around, this being a mostly residential section of the town. The odd person may take a picture with their smartphone if they cared to notice us, but the chances of a paparazzo finding us seemed remote.

"Do you think Max would mind if we took a walk on the

beach first?" I asked. "With such a pebbly shore line, I'm positive there must be some sea glass to be found here."

He took his phone out. "I'll text him and tell him we'll be there in about... how long?"

"Half an hour?"

He gave a nod and his thumbs went to work. Then we said goodbye to Nigel and found a set of stairs leading down to the stony beach.

"This cold won't let me stay out here long." I gasped as a particularly frigid gust permeated my jeans and thick sweater. We'd left the waxed jackets at home due to the clear forecast. "At least I know England is actually capable of a blue sky, though."

Jack took my hand. "So why the change of heart about being seen in public?"

I sighed and tried to organize my thoughts. After Charlotte and I had spoken last night, it was the first thing I'd thought about upon waking. Was my fear of the publicity forcing Jack to splinter apart his life and compartmentalize it even more? Making him feel, as Charlotte had suggested, emptier and emptier in his working life? If so, it was pretty much the most unfair thing I could do. And with all of his compartmentalizing, was it stopping him from becoming whole again, at peace with his past? We always connected perfectly in our sexual life, but was I really giving us a fair shot? I felt like coming here with Jack, meeting Max and supporting him in integrating a small part of his past life, was at least a step in the right direction.

"I'm not seeking it out, and this sleepy coastal town hardly counts as going out in public… but…"

Jack's arm closed around me and pulled me close as we walked. "But?"

"Maybe I've been a bit of a weirdo about it. I mean the sooner everyone gets used to seeing us together, the sooner it will become less of an issue. Not that they'll take photos of you less, but perhaps I won't feel like such a… specimen."

He laughed. "Yes, I do believe that's what I told you. Anyway, you've been totally gracious every time they do get in our faces. I think you'll find they can't help falling in love with you. There hasn't been one derogatory thing written about you since all the Audrey shit finally died down."

"How do you know? Do you look for stuff on me too?" I looked up from the stones beneath my feet.

He looked down at me. "The publicist keeps tabs for me… And now for 'us.'"

"Huh."

"What's huh?"

"Look, Jack. I know you've been protecting me kind of, and I totally appreciate it."

"It's for me too, you know. I don't relish being fodder all the time either."

"I know, but let me finish." I smiled at him. "I appreciate

you protecting me, it's what you promised to do. But perhaps it's making you feel like you're… kind of 'on your own' out there, while I sit safely in your non-movie life."

We stopped walking and turned to each other, and I looped my arms around his waist. "You've made a lot of changes for me, and perhaps I haven't made as many for you."

Jack's brow furrowed as his green eyes searched my face.

"You said some things last night—"

"I was drunk, I'm sorry." Jack's hand came up and raked through his hair.

"Don't be. I know this stuff has been on your mind, and maybe getting a bit wasted last night, helped you talk to me about how you were feeling."

"I was *feeling* horny." He chuckled.

I shook my head with a small grin. "You're incorrigible. But you were also feeling like you were the only one whose been fighting for us."

"It was a stupid thing to say. Again, I'm sorry."

"It wasn't a stupid thing to say. At all."

MAX TURNED OUT to be totally charming and down to earth. He had a kind, rounded, but very handsome face and was quick to smile and laugh. We joined him in a small screened off dining area at the back of the light-filled restaurant called Pier Nine. It was a beautiful space with original wood floors and lofty ceilings. "Classic Victorian elegance meets cool contemporary beach-chic," Max proudly intoned. The Christmas tree in one corner consisted of graduating lengths of driftwood stacked one on top of the other and draped with painted shells and white lights. It was *exactly* my style. I ran my mouth asking Max all about the operating of a small hotel/restaurant establishment.

The food, a modern take on fish and chips, was delicious, and despite being not all that hungry, Jack and I stuffed ourselves.

It was obvious Max thought the world of Jack, and confided to me over a lingering dessert of *Spotted Dick*—I left that one alone—and coffee, that *William Huntley* had been his best friend, and he'd never quite had another friend like him after Jack left school so suddenly at nine years old. Jack had swallowed heavily next to me and flushed along the tops of his cheekbones, but he didn't say a word. I thought it may have shocked him to silence.

Inwardly, I was happy with Max's confession. Maybe this would go someway toward helping Jack integrate his childhood with his life now, help him accept it as part of what made him who he was.

"Do you ever go back and see your school?" I asked suddenly, on a whim.

Jack tensed next to me, but I pretended not to notice, having voiced the question pleasantly to Max.

"Of course," Max responded cheerfully in his deep British baritone. "Always try and go back once a year and do a little tour. See how it's going. They're forever raising funds for this or that. Try to help, you know? Though boarding isn't quite what it used to be, it's more of a day school now."

"I'd like to go back and see it," said Jack.

I turned to him, surprised.

"Not many people will be there over the Christmas hols," said Max. "Just a skeleton crew. But I bet we could go next week. I'll probably have a lull in business after Christmas and Boxing Day."

"What's Boxing Day," I asked.

"The day after Christmas is a national holiday too," Jack said with a small smile like he'd just recovered the memory. "From the days when servants would receive a 'Christmas Box' and a day off from their masters or employers so they could, in turn, go and give a 'Christmas Box' to *their* families. A full-on remnant of the British gentry." His face clouded. Presumably Jack was thinking of his gentrified roots. Of his despicable father.

"So maybe the day after that then?" Max asked.

"Perfect," I chirped and squeezed Jack's knee under the table.

His hand grabbed mine and kept it in place. "Will you come with us?" Jack asked me seriously. His face was expressionless, but I knew it was a massive mental undertaking for him to go and face some of these early memories.

"Of course. I'd love to," I said casually but squeezed his knee hard to let him know how much I was there for him.

"Well, now." Max stretched and slapped his belly. "Don't suppose you have any single friends who are as charming as you looking for a nice English chap? Can we fly them over for New Year's? I don't have a date."

I couldn't believe Max didn't have a date.

"Her best friend is in love with her brother, so that's out," Jack answered for me.

"Oh, wow." Max's eyes grew wide. "So that incestuous interfamily relationship thing in those southern states is as bad as they make out. Thought it was just an overblown stereotype. And I thought the worst was cousins. Wow!"

I was stunned into confused silence, and Jack suddenly lost his shit—laughing so loud and hard, he had to scrape his chair back and put his head down, his arm wrapping around his midsection.

"What?" asked Max, nonplussed, and I finally let out a breathy laugh through my shock at the reactions of both

Jack, who apparently couldn't stop laughing, and Max, who was still shaking his head. Luckily, our dragged out meal had resulted in us being the last patrons of the establishment, so only a few curious servers popped their heads around the screen.

"Not her *own* brother," Jack wheezed, now literally crying.

"*My* brother." I laughed. "My best friend is in love with *my* brother."

"Ohhhh." Max's shoulders shook as he joined in Jack's mirth. "Ahh well, what about this new fad of movie stars falling in love with ordinary folks? Heard Evan Weston was the last down on the battlefield. Bloody loved his movie '*Retaliation*.'"

"Oh yeah, that was a good one. He's bad ass," Jack agreed.

"Any actresses you could hook me up with? I could have a little Notting Hill thing, but down here in Hastings."

We kept laughing and chatting for another hour or so until Max made mention of getting something and being right back. When he did, it was to hand an object wrapped in a napkin to Jack.

Jack took it with both hands and laid it on the white tablecloth in front of me.

"What?" I asked, confused.

Jack took the napkin away and left a small mason jar

filled with all different colors of sea glass. "Day seven gift," he murmured.

"Jack forgot this yesterday. The romantic schmuck spent all yesterday afternoon making me help him find bloody glass on the beach out there, didn't he?" Max said as if the idea was the most outlandish he'd taken part in.

The bowling ball-sized bubble full of weird emotion was back in my throat again, causing a blockage that made my eyes fill.

Jack slid his hand around the back of my neck and breathed a light kiss on my temple. "Don't cry," he whispered.

"Sorry." I sniffed and gave him and Max a watery smile. "Thank you. Thank you, both."

"You're welcome," said Max with a grunt. "Teaching me a thing or two. Just think. If he'd intercepted my romantic endeavors earlier, I may have had a girlfriend by now. As it is, I'm making it his priority to get me hooked up. Will you help?"

I laughed. "Yeah, I'll help."

"It's been a pleasure, Max," Jack told his friend. "Thank you. Keri Ann and I have The Grange to ourselves tonight, so we best be getting along to make use of it."

My cheeks went nuclear. *God, Jack.*

"Right-o, old chap. Say no more." Max hopped up. "I'll give you a shout about next week."

We said our good-byes and headed toward the rear exit where the parking was.

Jack stopped in the doorway leading out to the back patio, or *Candle-lit Garden* as Max had referred to it earlier, and pulled me into his embrace.

Looking around, making sure we weren't being watched, I then shot him a puzzled frown.

He was grinning down at me, and then lowered his face and caught my lips with his. "Mmm." He released me, and then reached up and stole a piece of greenery hanging in the tall doorframe.

"Jack, stop vandalizing the place," I teased.

"It's mistletoe. Now, mobile mistletoe. You never know when I might need it." He grinned boyishly, his dimple creasing his cheek, and stuck the foliage in his pocket. "Let's go home and get naked."

nine

IT WAS A heady feeling to have been out to lunch and driving back without worrying anyone was following us, or that we'd wake up to some crazy newspaper story tomorrow. Liberating really. "I adored meeting Max," I told Jack as we drove. "He's so nice. And I adored what he did with that building."

"Yeah, he's a good guy. I'm glad we're back in touch." Jack glanced in the side mirror and shifted the manual gear stick. He'd pushed his sleeves up and bared his forearms when he got in, and I was finding his handling of the car hard to tear my eyes away from. "What are you looking at?" he asked, glancing at me before setting his eyes back on the country lane.

"You have the sexiest forearms ever," I admitted.

"Forearms. You have a thing for my forearms? How did I never know this? I would have been brandishing them in front of you from day one."

I giggled. "You did."

"Wait. So this has been about my forearms all along?"

"Maybe." I shrugged and looked out at the scenery, trying to curb my stupid smile.

"Interesting," Jack mused. The car turned down the driveway to The Grange, and my heart beat faster as it came into view. "So, I just have to get this out the way and apologize."

Turning, I looked at him, questions clearly all over my face. "What for?"

Jack climbed out and came around to my side. He helped me out into the bright and cold afternoon and closed my door. Taking my face in his hands, he settled a long lingering kiss on my lips. "Because that's about the slowest thing I can manage right now," he informed me as he released my mouth, his eyes serious.

I released a breathy laugh, misting the cold air between us with condensation. "So even though this might mean we go even faster, I feel I should tell you something."

His eyebrows snapped together.

I bit my lip. "Well, um, I... ahem..." I chuckled awkwardly. "I went on the pill... finally. Merry Christmas."

Jack's chest caved, and his mouth dropped open. Then

closed. Then he swallowed loudly. "So," he croaked and cleared his throat. "Um—"

I grabbed his hand and pulled him toward the house.

It was his mom's house, and though we were alone, I felt we should probably confine ourselves to the bedroom out of deference. As soon as we were through the front door though, Jack had an arm around my waist and another tangled in my hair, angling my face just so. His hot mouth was on mine, and I opened to him, moaning as his tongue slid into me.

Vaguely, I heard his booted foot closing the front door behind us, and the light behind my eyelids dimmed. But mostly all I was conscious of was the taste of Jack and the trail of firing nerve endings left in the wake of one of his hands as it trailed down and cupped my ass, squeezing and pulling me hard against him. His soft hair was in a tight grip under my fingers as I drank in his kiss.

A long groan emanated from him, and we moved awkwardly toward the stairs.

Despite my release last night, I was vibrating with want within seconds. Jack had had no such release, and I felt it in his movements, his kisses, his breathing, and the grip of his hands. And I knew my news had added a probably unneeded fever pitch to his desire. His need only fueled the spark of my own, and within moments we were both caught in a torrent of fumbling, clutching, and desperate movements to get closer.

My sweater was whipped over my head and landed on

the floor. His followed. Then my hands were blindly pulling at the buttons on his jeans between us as I kissed him again.

I tried to stumble us backward so we could go to our room. My feet found the bottom step and I wrenched my mouth off Jack's, both of us gasping. Looking Jack in the eye, I stepped up two steps with a grin.

He followed and pulled me back in for another kiss, sliding his hand up under my long-sleeved thermal.

I pulled my mouth away and stepped up again.

His eyes were flinty in the dim light, and suddenly I found myself flipped around, my back pressed to his front and his breath in my ear. I gasped at the sudden movement.

"I want you so badly," he growled, and his hands were under my shirt, kneading my breasts, roaming my belly and snapping my jeans undone. His actions were jerky and feverish, and the idea that he was losing complete control undid me.

I cried out as his hand pushed into my jeans and between my legs.

"Fuck," he groaned as his fingers found me ready for him.

Breath was hard to come by, and my chest heaved as my body ached and throbbed. Completely lost in the moment, I helped him push down my jeans to my thighs and reached behind me to help him. Seconds later my hands were on a worn wood stair tread, and I screamed loudly as Jack pushed his hard length into me.

"Holy shit," Jack choked out. "Baby, I'm sorry, shit."

I had no words. Did he think he'd hurt me? Maybe he had, the ecstasy and arousal was so sharp it was painful. But the feel of him inside me, with nothing between us, was almost too much to think about without losing it. Did he feel the same? I rocked back, only able to articulate a keening and needy sound at the raw sensation.

"Oh, God." Jack hissed and took my movement and returned it. "You feel so good. I can't..."

"More," I was finally able to whisper.

He thrust into me, and I thrust back desperate for more. For him. For everything he had. And he gave it. His hands gripped my hips, my hair, my breasts. The loss of his control, his roughness, the knowledge of how much he craved me, threw me toward a shattering climax within seconds.

I tensed, my knuckles white on the step as the shattering wave rolled through me. I knew when Jack felt it, I knew when he let go too, joining me in wave after wave of it. The sound he made seared into my heart.

The entire thing was over in minutes, and we were in a tangled sweaty heap against the stairs.

Not even halfway up.

I giggled even as I tried to catch my breath.

Jack laughed too, dropping a clammy forehead to my

neck. "Wow," he breathed and dropped a kiss to the sensitive skin below my ear. "Um. Sorry?"

"Don't be sorry. That was… uh, intense."

"No shit." He drew away and pulled me with him, helping haul my jeans back up. Then I was in his arms, being carried up the stairs. "Let's move this to a bed."

WE SPENT THE rest of the afternoon and most of the evening in bed. Jack couldn't seem to get over the feeling of being inside me. "I think," he said at one point, as he lay cradled between my legs, inside me but not moving, "I'll just stay like this forever."

"I guess you could do voice-over work," I deadpanned.

"Yes," he stated with surprise at my incredible idea. "Fantastic."

"But what will *I* do?"

"You mean you don't want to just lie there doing nothing?"

"Ha ha."

He started to rock inside me gently. "Even when it feels like this?"

I bit my lip.

He dropped his head, curving his back so his mouth

could reach my breast. The angle caused his hips to grind more fully into me.

My breathing stumbled.

"Or like this," he murmured, flicking his tongue over my nipple and catching it lightly with his teeth.

"Well, when you put it that way," I gasped. I drew my legs up and wrapped them around his back.

Jack's eyes found mine, dark lids lowered, a smirk playing round his mouth. "I love you, Keri Ann," he said, his smile falling from his mouth. "So much."

I closed my eyes briefly, drawing his words into me. "I love you too, Jack."

"Do those words ever seem inadequate for how you feel?"

"Always," I answered.

Levering his upper body up, he took my hands palm to palm and pressed them into the mattress. His knees found purchase and he rocked deeper into me. The bed squeaked and groaned under our movements. My ankles stayed locked around him.

"One day," he rasped, the flush of arousal glowed from his skin and darkened his eyes. "One day, when I'm inside you and I let go, I'm going to be thinking about the magic of creating a baby inside you and how me loving you like this can create something so amazing."

The depth of emotion on his face, in his eyes, had me

swallowing my heart back down my throat.

"I want that with you one day, Keri Ann. I want everything with you."

My chest filled up at his words. Even though I knew his use of the words, *one day*, belied the fact he was thinking of it even now, I knew he would wait with me. Wait until I was ready. Until *we* were ready. It was such a *certain* feeling, I wondered why I'd freaked out yesterday morning when I thought he was bringing our future up.

"I want everything with you too, Jack," I vowed and imagined I could see the promise enter his heart.

We moved together gently.

Rocking slowly.

Breathing as one.

And falling in tandem.

"IT'S CHRISTMAS," I squealed. "And it's snowing. Wake up!"

Jack groaned and rolled over next to me. I was sitting up in the small twin bed in the Blue Room peering out the window next to me. The landscape was bleached white under a thin layer of snow while more flurried against the windows. "Merry Christmas, Dork," he chuckled sleepily.

"Your dork," I corrected.

"Yes," he conceded. "All mine."

Since Charlotte and Jeff had returned from London a few days ago, we'd taken to sleeping wrapped around each other in the single Blue Room bed since we discovered it was solid as a rock and didn't make a sound. Although, *we* still couldn't make any noise. It had made for an intense few stolen moments over the days leading up to Christmas.

"It's snowing! How can you not be excited about that? I've never seen snow. I've never even seen it falling. I've never touched it."

Jack opened his eyes and squinted. "Seriously?"

"Seriously," I said.

"Well, shit." He sat up, the sheet falling to reveal his beautiful naked chest, then swung his legs out the side. "We better remedy that immediately."

"Thaaaank you," I drawled with a massive grin, pleased he was finally getting the importance of the situation. I planted a kiss between his shoulder blades.

We flung our clothes on, and I took the stairs two at a time, almost breaking my neck when I slipped three from the bottom. Luckily Jack was right behind me and grabbed my sweater in a lightning fast reflex. "Bloody hell, you minx. You just scared the living crap out of me. Slow down already."

"Listen to you, so *bloody* British. Thank you, Sir Jack," I quipped, but my heart pounded from my near disaster.

We bundled into our wellies and Barbour jackets, and

Jack grabbed our gloves out of the basket by the front door.

I was literally a giddy child on Christmas morning as I flung open the front door into the blast of cold winter morning.

Jack hauled me back into the doorframe mid-rush and planted a kiss on my lips.

"What?" I asked impatiently.

"Mistletoe," he mumbled, nodding to where he'd tacked it above the front door. "Won't ever pass it up."

God, he was cute.

I huffed and grinned at him, then dragged him by the hand outside and around the house, marveling at the tracks of our boots pressed into the fresh unmarred snow. I let go his hand and turned in a slow three sixty. "We're in a snow globe," I whispered with awe. For a moment, I stopped and stood there feeling the icy pings drop as they flared briefly on my skin and melted to water.

"Taste them," Jack said and tilted his head back and put his tongue out.

Laughing, I did the same. The tiny frigid drops pinged on my tongue. They melted to a minuscule amount of water, and the flavor was vaguely… dusty. "Well, they don't taste as awesome as they look," I said.

"Hmm, a uniquely, coal-mining-town flavor," said Jack. "With a northern flair. Newcastle, perhaps?"

"Well, the water evaporates into the air from

somewhere," I said with a chuckle. "You could be right."

Jack leaned down and used two hands to scrape some snow together, leaving an exposed strip of dark grass. "Now, if it's sticky snow, we're in luck."

"Why's that?" I asked, and then registered the mischief in his eyes. "Oh no you don't," I squealed and turned and ran toward the lawn at the front of the house.

Jack followed at a slow amble, packing his snowball and giving me time to scrape my own together. I was useless, and he had perfect aim. The first one hit me square in the chest, exploding cold snow over my neck and down into my collar.

"Yikes," I screeched. "That's cold."

I raced toward him instead of throwing my ball, and as soon as he caught me in a hug, I attempted to stuff the snowball down the neck of his jacket. We wrestled, falling to the ground. We were laughing our heads off and grabbing determined fistfuls of snow, most of which ended up in each other's faces before they had a chance to breech each other's protective clothing.

Finally, we were cold and starving for breakfast and made our way inside, stamping our boots at the door. Jack stole another kiss from me in the doorway, and we floated back into the warmth of the house. The smell of coffee, cinnamon, and pine logs smoldering in the living room fireplace caused a huge wave of happiness to wash over me. It was almost time for presents.

ten

"MORNING YOU TWO. Merry Christmas." Charlotte nodded at us with a smile and blew over her tea. "Go on and sit by the Aga. Warm up before we exchange gifts."

"Merry Christmas," we both greeted them. We were damp and cold from our snowball fight.

Charlotte looked fantastic, as she always did. Her dark hair was pulled back in a low ponytail and even makeup-free she was beautiful. She wore a set of red, green, and blue button-down plaid pajamas.

Jeff vacated his seat near the Aga, motioning Jack and me to sit down. An early bird, he was already dressed in worn jeans and a cream Aran sweater. "Come on. Sit down. Tea or coffee? You both look frozen. Happy, but frozen."

Happy.

So freaking happy.

For the first time since I was a child, I felt a sense of utter completeness. I know I wasn't spending Christmas with Joey, or even seeing Jazz for that matter. Nana was gone, and Mrs. Weaton had been invited by Paulie at the Grill to spend Christmas with his extended family up in Okatie. But somehow, without even knowing how much I needed it, I'd found something better than I'd ever imagined. I was in a family. Jack's family. Did Jack understand how lucky he was? Because I felt very, very lucky.

"Tea for me, please." I was becoming addicted to the stuff. I had a predisposition to tea, being from the south, but this was served hot, not iced, and I was beginning to crave it.

"Coffee," said Jack. "Thank you."

Jack's gifts over the last few days had gotten a little more grandiose, but I was trusting he wouldn't pull out an engagement ring this morning. The day after Hastings, he told me he'd adopted a sea turtle in my name at the Sea Turtle Rescue Center on Jekyll Island, in coastal Georgia. Three mornings ago, he'd given me a gold bangle with a small collection of charms hanging off it that Jack said were symbolic of our relationship. There was a sea turtle, a tiny piece of sea glass, and a circular pendant that had J&KA stamped on it. It was so pretty. I adored it and had worn it almost every moment since.

The next day he'd presented me with a bundle of papers

tied in a red grosgrain ribbon. Before he let me undo them, he'd sat me down in front of the fireplace in the living room with a mug of Brandy eggnog. He talked about Max's place and how amazing it was when historical homes were turned into places the modern traveler could visit. He was a renovation buff, so I totally bought his interest in the concept, even though I was confused by his weird tangent. The papers turned out to be the tax liens against the Butler Family home. Jack had paid them all off and had them released so we could stop worrying about losing the house for a while.

I freaked out, as he knew I would. So he'd gently suggested I consider a concept like Max had done with the place in Hastings and regard Jack as an investor. It totally shut me up because the whole time Max had been talking, I'd been fantasizing what it would be like to do a similar thing with the Butler house one day. Jazz was studying Hospitality and Business. Perhaps she'd help. How would my brother Joey react, though?

Christmas Eve day, Jack presented me with airplane tickets to a Caribbean island. Apparently we were going halfway home for New Year's Eve. That gift was tricky, because while it sounded incredible and I was super excited, I also knew Max would adore it if Jack spent New Year's at Pier Nine, in Hastings. And I wasn't sure, but I felt certain Charlotte and Jeff thought we were staying.

And that brought us up to today's gift. To be honest, I

didn't know how he could top snow.

Charlotte sliced some fruitcake onto a serving plate and added some brandy butter on the side. "This is normally a decadent dessert," she informed me with a wink. "But I say breakfast deserves a little something special today. Anyway, we have the Everseas and Nigel coming for lunch, as well as a work colleague of Jeff's who lost his wife this year. Turkey's already in, and we've a ton of food. So we need to save a bit of an appetite."

"Smells delicious." I inhaled deeply and walked the plate to the living room where we all settled by the fire. Our presents were all nesting under the boughs of the small elegant Christmas tree to the side of the fireplace.

Charlotte had been helping me the last few days with the finishing touches on my present for Jack, while Jeff had enlisted him to help rebuild one side of Charlotte's chicken coop that had been getting weak. I couldn't wait to see what Jack thought of my unconventional gift.

"Who'll be Father Christmas?" Charlotte asked. She was holding a furry red hat trimmed in white wool.

I nudged Jack. "I'm assuming she means Santa. I have to see you in that."

"No way."

"I'll do it," Jeff said officiously and pulled it on. "It's an important job."

A vision of Charlotte and Jeff as grandparents to our

children suddenly caught me by surprise. I remembered Jack's words when making love to me, and warmth hit me straight in the womb. My insides flipped with emotion, and my eyes pricked. I reached for Jack's hand and squeezed, causing him to glance at me quizzically.

Whatever he saw in my eyes had him turning fully toward me. He brought his hand to my cheek as I stared deep into his green eyes and wondered how on earth my life had ended up here in this room, with these beautiful people, and so much love and hope that my entire future seemed bursting with promise.

Jack watched me like he knew what was going on in my head. Like he'd been waiting for me to get there. Then he dropped his forehead to mine. "One day," he whispered.

Charlotte perched herself on the wing chair, but not before turning the radio on low volume to caroling Christmas music.

"All right," said Jeff and slid his eyeglasses down to the very tip of his nose to read a gift tag on a small package. "Dearest Mum, Merry Christmas, love, Jack and Keri Ann."

I had helped Jack wrap the gorgeous scarf, like mine, but in soft blue-grey. Jeff handed her the package to open.

"Oh, it's gorgeous," Charlotte gushed, brushing her cheek against the exquisite material. It looked incredible against her skin tone. "Now Jack, this is not some endangered species is it? It feels even softer than cashmere. There's that endangered animal in the Himalayas, the Sha-something."

"The *Shahtoosh*. Mum, you know me better than that. It's vicuña. All responsible, I promise."

"Well, thank you. It's stunning."

Jeff got a pair of fur-lined slippers and a dressing gown, for his "retirement," from Jack and me. But personally from me, Jeff got a small fun hardback book that contained the craziest lawsuits ever filed in America, which he absolutely adored, and kept reading excerpts so Jack had to take over Santa duties. As expected, Jack looked cute as heck. Just what I wanted for Christmas.

I gave Charlotte an angel Christmas tree ornament I'd handmade from bleached oyster shells, Spanish Moss, and sea glass. She immediately hung it and saved the box to carefully pack it back into for next year.

Jack handed me a long wrapped poster tube, his face so full of boyish excitement, I couldn't help grinning.

"Dearest Keri Ann," I read. "All my love, Jack."

I tore the paper off and opened the end of the tube, sliding the rolled up contents out. Pulling them open, I realized I was looking at site plans and architectural drawings and legal papers. "What is this?" I asked, confused.

Jack took them and helped spread them out on the coffee table, and then pointed to a bottom corner of a site plan.

Daufuskie Island, Lots 21 & 22, Waterfront,
Butler-Eversea construction project.

"Oh my God," I squealed. We were insanely in love with that island and had already amassed some pretty incredible memories there within the last six months. "Did you find a place on the island? Are you building?"

"We are," he said, grinning. "It's in our joint names, and I've found an architect and given him some of these drawings, but I need you to design your own studio space."

"Holy shit," I said. "Oops, sorry." I grimaced, looking at Jeff and Charlotte, but they just laughed at me.

"Well?" Jack asked. "Good holy shit, or bad holy shit?"

"Good on one condition," I said. "Jeff and Charlotte have to promise right now to come and visit us the moment it's completed."

"Of course," Charlotte answered.

"Wouldn't miss it," added Jeff with a smile.

Jack gave a small grin. "So you love it?" I didn't miss his flicker of concern.

It wasn't an engagement ring. It was an even more extravagant and binding future. And it meant him in the Lowcountry and us together. I threw my arms around his neck, knocking off the Santa hat. "I love it!"

JACK SELECTED THE next thick square package from under the tree. The package I had carefully placed there yesterday.

"For me." He looked up at me. "From you."

"Yep." I was nervous. I had no idea what to get Jack that was meaningful to him. Figuring out gifts for people was always hard. But for Jack? Impossible. If the guy wanted something, he bought it.

He brought it over and sat next to me as he tore the blue and silver wrapping. Pulling the paper away, he revealed a thick scrapbook. I could tell he was confused. Especially when he opened the first page and staring up at him was a tabloid article with the words "Where in the World is Jack?" It was over a year old, right in the middle of his scandal with Audrey. He tensed next to me, his brow furrowed. I sensed Charlotte watching him cautiously from across the room.

"What is this?" he asked, his voice oddly raspy.

"Keep going," I whispered.

He turned the page to where I'd pasted in a carefully handwritten sheet of paper, and his eyes scanned my words:

Standing in front of me was the most beautiful man I had seen in all of my twenty-two years on this planet. His rich dark brown hair,

mussed up from the hat, stood up in a few places and framed a hard-
planed face set with eyes the color of...

Well, I really couldn't tell the color of his eyes in the shadows, but I
knew exactly what color they were, a deep grey-green. I hadn't been hiding
under a rock for the last five years. And I certainly didn't need to double
check the tabloid magazine Jazz had been reading, which definitely did
not do him justice, to know that standing in front of me, Keri Ann
Butler, outside the Snapper Grill in Butler Cove, population nine
thousand, and hundreds of miles away from his expected location in
Hollywood, was none other than Jack Eversea.

"I still don't understand."

"Keep going, please."

Jack smiled tightly.

Next were even more articles, but this time my addition
to the time period was a note he'd left me and his shopping
list he'd texted me that I screen grabbed and printed out. That
was followed by some more of our bantering texts.

Then on the day of Audrey's released statement about
her and Jack's breakup, I'd pasted in a copy of the receipt
where he'd paid to have the floors done at my house, followed
by a handwritten entry that made me blush to read it,
describing our first kiss and first intimate moments.

Jack was pale and swallowed heavily. But he kept turning
pages and reading. I'd put in the reports about him being seen
in Savannah with Audrey, which was a painful time for both

of us to remember. And for those pages, I'd put in personal recollections of Jack. I'd written about my conversation with my brother and his observation of how Jack looked at me.

Like you were the last chopper out of Baghdad, the last IV in the field hospital, the last funnel cake at the fair...

I just know that the way he was looking at you, he's coming back someday.

There were reports of a massive showdown between Jack and Audrey, and Jack's agent being fired. I wrote about my birthday, and seeing Devon, and how I'd felt meeting him. My worry for Jack and what his agent and Audrey may have done to hurt him. The fear that Jack wouldn't come back, that what we'd felt was in my own imagination.

It was painful, especially when I got to the parts where he was in England, and there were photos of him with random girls. I bared my soul writing about the day I'd tortured myself with Internet pictures of him for hours and how Jazz had ripped the modem from the wall.

Jack was dead silent, paging through our intimately personal history, his hand trembling slightly, learning things about us, about me, that changed the memories captured by the tabloids.

But I'd also found, thanks to Charlotte, a few lesser circulated stories about his work on the movie and how there was talk of it being an award show nomination. In a crazy twist of fate, on the same day those stories had been published, I'd received my acceptance letter to SCAD. I pasted it in alongside.

I know I'll think about Jack every day for the rest of my life. He changed me. He made me want more. Made me want to be more. Those are good things. I'm hanging onto them.

I talked about Colt asking me out.

Colt made me happy. He made me laugh. What was wrong with me? Was it still too soon, or was it that Jack Eversea was a fire that burned brighter than the sun, and I'd been seared beyond repair?

I pasted in the invitation to be part of the summer exhibition of Southern artists at the Westin on Hilton Head Island. And I pasted in a few photocopied pieces of Jack's journal that he'd shared with me. The next page was a picture I'd taken of Jack riding a horse shirtless on the beach, and a picture I'd stolen from his phone of me from that same day.

On the day Audrey's crazy lost pregnancy story broke, I added the newspaper story of the auction and how Jack had ended up in a bidding war for a student's work. *Mine.*

And then came the tabloid pictures of us together, some with less than savory headlines. With every one of them, I wrote a small anecdote of what we were doing on the day they were published. Funny or beautiful things Jack had said to me that I remembered, or tickets to things we'd done, a flyer for the cottage rental place on Daufuskie where we always tried to steal time together.

Even though I knew Jack had a copy, I added in the

story that reporter Shannon Keith had written about Jack and me and how we met. Some of the final pictures were of us at the airport in Atlanta and at Heathrow where we'd landed and where the stupid photographers had yelled out disgusting things. I pasted our boarding tickets in and wrote *Keri Ann's first flight across the ocean* and *The day Keri Ann learned what the word SNOG means*. There was a postcard from Hastings and finally a colored pencil sketch of a bull chasing a boy and a girl with a red scarf.

You are my star, I wrote, *I'd follow you anywhere.*

There were still pages left to fill at some point. I hadn't even put in my first experience with snow.

The room was deathly quiet, and I realized Jeff and Charlotte had left. Jack was still holding the book, his knuckles now white, and staring at the last page so I couldn't see the expression on his face.

Shit.

Heart pounding with terror, I swallowed some moisture back into my mouth and slid off the couch to kneel in front of him. "Please say something." I was barely able to form words.

"I can't," Jack whispered, still staring at the book. Then he carefully closed it and moved it off his lap next to him. His Adam's apple bobbed roughly in his throat and his nostrils flared. A pulse beat visibly at his temple, and I realized he was trying to compose himself. He raised his face and his eyes were vivid and full, the green sparkling to depths I'd never seen. It was wonder, it was love, it was a thousand things I couldn't name.

He reached out and took my face in his warm rough hands. "You," Jack said on a choked up whisper, shaking his head slightly. Moments passed where we looked into each other, and he didn't say anything more. Then his thumb brushed over my lips. "You," he said finally, "make... *every... single... thing* in my world beautiful."

the end

thank you

The first people I wish to thank are my readers without whom this novella would never have been possible. You fell in love with Jack, just like I did. Your messages, your encouragement and your support continue to mean so much to me everyday; on the best days and especially the difficult days.

Thank you to my Assistant, Julie Burke, who has the thankless task of trying to keep me organized (so if you ordered or won a book, requested a turtle tattoo, or just needed an answer for something – and got it? Chances are Julie reminded me). The list goes on though: teasers? She made them. Facebook banners? Yep. Inside scoop on Clare and Jamie/ #SamCat? Yep. Staying up until 2 am to watch The Wedding Episode with me? She's awesome. AND she's an incredible person to boot.

And Lisa Wilhelm, my wonderful friend, supporter and Street Team admin (along with Julie), purveyor of color-coded candy and supplies (all in my favorite color). You're amazing. I'm so lucky to know you. Thank you for everything you so.

Kate Roth. When you said you'd bundle a Christmas novella with me you made my year. And your cover is stunning! Thank you for being so talented and so fun to work with.

Judy Roth, my editor, who always makes my work shine. And Dave and Al, who are hard task masters and bring out my best. Tuesdays are my favorite day of the week. I miss seeing you both face to face.

And as always thanks go to my husband and sons. Without their support this would all be impossible.

Keep in touch! I'd love to hear from you!

Facebook: www.facebook.com/authornatashaboyd

Pinterest: www.pinterest.com/lovefrmlowcntry

Twitter: @lovefrmlowcntry

Instagram: @lovefrmlowcntry

Tumblr: eversea.tumblr.com

Also by Natasha Boyd

Eversea

Forever, Jack

All That Jazz

and

Deep Blue Eternity

Made in the USA
Columbia, SC
08 January 2021

30516540R00072